Dead Man's Cañon

Center Point
Large Print

Also by Lauran Paine and available from
Center Point Large Print:

Kansas Kid
Trail of Shadows
Night of the Rustler's Moon
Wagon Train West
Iron Marshal
Six-Gun Crossroads

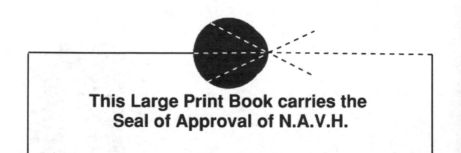

**This Large Print Book carries the
Seal of Approval of N.A.V.H.**

Dead Man's Cañon

Lauran Paine

CENTER POINT LARGE PRINT
THORNDIKE, MAINE

This Circle Ⓥ Western is published by
Center Point Large Print in the year 2017 in
co-operation with Golden West Literary Agency.

First Edition
April, 2017

Printed in the United States of America
on permanent paper.
Set in 16-point Times New Roman type.

ISBN: 978-1-68324-351-9

Library of Congress Cataloging-in-Publication Data

Names: Paine, Lauran, author.
Title: Dead man's cañon : a Circle V western / Lauran Paine.
Description: First edition. | Thorndike, Maine : Center Point Large Print,
2017.
Identifiers: LCCN 2016059362 | ISBN 9781683243519
    (hardcover : alk. paper)
Subjects: LCSH: Large type books. | GSAFD: Western stories.
Classification: LCC PS3566.A34 D427 2017 | DDC 813/.54—dc23
LC record available at https://lccn.loc.gov/2016059362

Chapter One

This time of year the roads were excellent. Dry, hard, rutted, and dusty, with some traffic, mostly stages going as far as Rockland on the border, then back up north again, so if a man chose another route he'd have his private reasons. Or, as Claude Rainey, sheriff of Apache County said often enough, when a man chose the Gila monster, rattlesnake, and tarantula country off to the east, for entering Arizona out of Mexico, only a fool would assume he had nothing to hide.

Just how right Rainey turned out to be came to light the 1st of April, two months earlier, when some Hightower cowboys, hunting strayed horses, came upon the mummified corpse of a man and his horse over along the north slope of one of those lonely cañons that ran like large funnels straight down to the border, and broadened out across the line down into Mexico, becoming the Tamaulipas Plains.

But Claude Rainey's statement about men slipping over the line because they had something to hide meant that they were the hiders—those lonely men who rode the barren trails. It didn't mean they literally wanted to hide something, which is where the double play on words came in, because those Hightower cowboys found something within fifty feet of where that dead man lay. He'd obviously come up out of Mexico to that god-forsaken place where he'd died, to dig the hole, place the box in it, then cover the hole and walk fifty feet before someone shot the top off his head, then gave his horse a third eye.

There was nothing on the body, no letters, no newspapers, not even a name inked inside the expensive gray Stetson hat. No one would have recognized him after a month of lying out there under a sun that burned everything a chocolate color after fifteen days anyway, even if his face hadn't been hopelessly stretched all out of shape by the bullet that killed him.

Hightower's foreman, Al Trail, backtracked as best he could but no one down in any of those little Mex towns over the line had ever seen anyone answering the dead man's description. That surprised no one, either. Border villages south of the line existed only because American outlaws brought their money down there. It would indeed be an ungrateful—and foolish—*cantina* keeper or a *vaquero* who would point a finger at any of those *gringo* desperadoes. It would also, in all probability, be fatal. The fact that one man had died didn't mean he mightn't have friends who'd look darkly on any mention of him to strangers.

So Trail rode back to Springville, made Sheriff Claude Rainey buy him three cool beers for his trouble, and said there was nothing known—or at least said—about the mysterious stranger, over the line in Mexico.

Ordinarily none of this would have been necessary. The town of Springville had a Boot Hill cemetery just like every other border town also had. There were four solid rows of headboards with UNKNOWN painted across them. One more wouldn't make one bit of difference—except for that box the Hightower cowboys had dug up and handed over to Sheriff Rainey when they brought word of the corpse out there in the grassless, treeless, brushless, wide and lonely cañon. It had five packets of bloodstained $100 bills in it.

Sheriff Rainey confided sourly that if those damned cowboys of Al Trail's had just taken the money and said nothing about the corpse, or better yet, had buried it, Rainey would have been delighted. Trail said, with a broad smile, that the only reason they hadn't done just exactly that, was because they figured it out, and to dig a grave in that iron-like, summer-hardened gritty soil, big enough to hide the man and his dead horse, was just plain worth more money.

Trail had been teasing, of course, and Rainey knew it. Those five packets of $100 bills, with the blood on them, were thick enough to choke an alligator. There was $10,000 in spendable cash in that box, more money than nine-tenths of the men in Arizona Territory had ever seen in one pile, in one place, in their lives. The only logical excuse those horse-hunting Hightower cowboys'd had for bringing in that box, was that they were honest men.

Rainey told that to Al Trail at the bar. He also told it to the U.S. marshal who came on the south-bound coach from Tucson in response to Rainey's letter. And finally, Claude told it to Newton Douglas, the man who owned more of the town of Springville than anyone else, and who also ran more cattle on the northerly desert than anyone else. Rainey also told Douglas that unless he sure was guessing wide, that fellow had stolen the box full of cash and was running with it, when someone he'd either stolen it from, or who he'd double-crossed to get the money, caught up with him in that blast-furnace cañon, and killed him.

Then Newton Douglas asked the same question Al Trail had also asked. "Why, since they killed him for it, didn't they take the damned box with 'em when they left?"

Claude Rainey had no answer to that. Neither did anyone else. In fact, that's what became the biggest riddle of all.

The facts that the dead man had been young and in his prime, had been riding a good horse, and was wearing a stag-handled six-gun, were completely lost sight of. What everyone preferred to speculate about was why, after he'd killed the mysterious stranger, hadn't he dug up that box full of bloodstained money?

There were ten dozen reasons advanced, and not a one of them made a lick of sense. As Al Trail said, after they'd planted the nameless dead man: "There just can't be any good excuse . . . unless someone killed that man without giving a damn about his money."

That was hard to swallow, of course, since everyone liked $10,000. Al shook his head over that. "Nope. Go look at that stuff over in Barney Whitsun's safe at the general store. Blood on it. Now someone put that blood on there, and someone . . . whoever killed the stranger . . . wasn't trying to rob the dead man. He was out to avenge that blood."

It was as good a theory as any other. Claude Rainey said he was satisfied with it. But he also said: "Just what am I supposed to do . . . keep that money in Barney's safe forever?"

Trail had the answer to that one, also. "Just sit back, Claude. Just sit back and wait. At least one man knows where that money was. Sooner or later someone's going to ride into Springville looking for it. Sooner or later . . . someone will come."

Barney Whitsun's store, up the road two buildings from the jailhouse and on the opposite side of the road, was the favorite hang-out for cowmen and range riders of the desert country. There was a saloon on up the roadway, north-ward, run by Jack Mather, a big, swarthy, laughing man with a badly re-set broken nose and scarred

9

eyebrows, but at least part of the time loafers hung out down at Barney's place.

After Barney had that bloodstained $10,000 in his steel safe, he had more loafers than ever.

Once, when he met Claude Rainey over at the café that adjoined—and was owned by the same man who owned the hotel, Springville's only hotel—Barney said he wished Claude would find some other place for that money, that while it brought him a lot more folks, they didn't buy anything, they simply cluttered up the store and endlessly argued about the money.

But there was no other place, unless Sheriff Rainey put it under his mattress, because Barney had the only real steel safe in Apache County. In fact, Barney had the only genuine general store in Apache County. There were other villages, mostly Mexican, and other stores, but none that carried Barney Whitsun's inventory of goods. A man could buy a pint of liniment or a new N. Porter saddle at Whitsun's place. He could buy guns of all makes and calibers, ammunition for everyone, and he could also buy bolt goods to placate the squaw when he'd been out all night.

Barney had a thriving business; the idlers, as he'd said, rarely bought anything greater than a 5¢ sack of Bull Durham tobacco, yet they stood in the coolness of the old building, leaning on the counters, and interfered with Barney's real customers.

Sheriff Rainey sat and sweated over at his jail-house with the roadway door open in case a breeze happened along, and pondered. He'd had one hour with the U.S. marshal; they'd talked; the marshal had examined the dead man's gun, his saddle, bridle, and blanket, then he'd got on the next stage heading south and that was the last Claude had seen of him. Worst of all, he'd been a lanky, red-headed man with a mouth like a bear trap who grunted occasionally, but never volunteered a word unless Claude had dragged it up out of him. That left Claude exactly where he'd been before—in the dark.

The second week after they'd buried the mummified corpse Al Trail was at Mather's bar when Claude walked in and jokingly said he'd heard the Mexican government was going to send someone from one of those Mexican border armies up after that $10,000.

Claude had snapped his answer right back. "Suits me fine. I'll even meet 'em at the edge of town and hand the damned box over. Be that glad to get shed of it."

The dead horse still lay where he'd fallen. Claude rode out for a final look, and where badgers had tunneled under the carcass for their feast, Claude saw something. Part of an old brand burned into the dead horse's lower left stifle.

He got down, kicked the hide around until he got a fair look, then drew a reproduction of the

11

mark in his notebook, and very thoughtfully drifted back into town before most folks had even missed him.

There was no telegraph office at Springville, but the stage company often carried private letters for Claude when he wanted fast service. He wrote a letter to the Registrar of Brands over at Phoenix, made a faithful drawing of the mark on that dead horse, asked for all the available information, sealed the letter, and took it up to the stage company office where a clerk said it would go out with the very next north-bound coach.

That made Rainey feel much better. Until those badgers had co-operated he hadn't had a single thing to go on. The next afternoon when he encountered Al Trail over at Hank Smith's shoeing shop, he took Al's quiet ribbing in good humor and said he thought, if no one showed up to claim that $10,000 pretty quick, he'd appropriate it in the name of Springville, and get a school built with it.

That same night, up at Mather's bar, which had a sign outside proclaiming the place as The Springville Oasis, he ran into Newton Douglas. Newton was a large, spare, dry man in his late sixties, who'd come to the border country as a young man—some said with a posse close behind him—and who'd been working hard ever since. He wasn't talkative except with a few men, of whom Claude Rainey was one, and he so seldom smiled or laughed folks said that's how often it rained in Springville and the desert country—only when Newton Douglas smiled.

But there was a twinkle in his eyes this evening; he knew how the Hightower bunch had been ragging Claude over his private mystery and the $10,000, so, as he signaled Jack Mather to bring down another drink for the sheriff, he said: "Claude, there's some kind of a law . . . bound to be one . . . that lets folks put a claim on money no one is willing to say belongs to them. Now I was thinking, if we split it down the middle and . . ."

"Newt," said Rainey softly, breaking into the other man's drawled speech, "I've got a better idea. Let's build a school for Springville with that money."

Claude wasn't joking. He'd been joking down at the blacksmith shop, but he wasn't joking now, because he'd had all afternoon to think it over. The more he pondered, the better he liked the notion. So now, with Newton Douglas, he wasn't joking at all.

"A school with a cupola on it with a good bronze bell up there, all painted white with one big room and real desks, and a fine pair of His and Hers out back, along with some sheds and corrals for the ranch kids to leave their horses in."

Claude stopped talking. Jack Mather was listening to him over the bar. Newton Douglas

13

was gazing at him, all the hint of humor gone. Throughout the barroom men turned and gazed at him. Springville didn't have a school; it hadn't ever had one. The children now studied in the harness maker's back room.

Chapter Two

The mysterious stranger was well in his grave and even some of the loafers had stopped hanging around Barney Whitsun's store by the time that tall Mexican rode into Springville, looking for Sheriff Rainey.

He asked about Claude up at the Oasis late in the afternoon when there was a fair-size crowd of range men at the bar hiding from the sun blast, so it only took moments for word to sweep up and down through town that a big Mex was looking for Claude, probably to lay claim to the town's $10,000.

Claude was over at Newton Douglas's cow camp six miles west of town and didn't return until the sun had set, which was the best time to travel the desert if one couldn't postpone his trip until just before sunup, which was an even better time.

By the time Claude got back to town and put up his horse everyone knew about the tall Mexican, except Claude, and he learned of him almost before he'd stepped down from the saddle.

The Mexican had already eaten at the café and was drowsing on the bench outside Rainey's jailhouse in night's long layer of desert gloom by the time Claude caught up with him. He introduced himself, sat down, and offered the big Mex his makings. The stranger refused, lighting up one of those foul little black cigars of his country, instead.

He was a handsome man, young and poised with fine features and expressive large eyes. He said his name was Fernando Bríon, that he ranched quite some distance below the border in Tamaulipas state, and he had some effects for Sheriff Rainey which he'd preferred to deliver personally. Then, from inside his short *charro* jacket, Fernando Bríon brought forth a six-gun with a stag handle, a gold watch and chain with the name Jonas Gantt engraved on the inside of the front cover, a wallet with both U.S. and Mex money in it, and—finally—a U.S. marshal's badge.

Claude sat looking at the stuff. He picked up the badge and fingered it for a while. So that's why he had never again seen that federal marshal.

Bríon said softly: "All I can tell you, *señor*, is that he was shot by someone no one saw. South of the border we think, since there are many *Americanos*, he was probably killed by some *pistolero* he was tracking down. It has never been wise for lawmen to come down to Tamaulipas from the *Estados Unidos*." Bríon gave a little shrug. "Of course this one wasn't wearing his badge. It was in his pocket. But these men know one another. Outlaws and lawmen have a private

16

world, Sheriff . . . they know one another, usually."

Claude picked up the dead man's belongings. He'd scarcely known Jonas Gantt. The only time they'd met, Gantt had sat like stone making only an occasional grunt in response to Claude's questions. It wasn't Gantt's killing that disturbed Claude so much as it was the fact that evidently Gantt had been after someone, probably the murderer of the mummified stranger, when he'd been assassinated. That meant the $10,000 very probably had living heirs. Then Bríon casually made a statement that brought Claude's eyes around to him in a rush.

He said: "I would've brought back his saddle and bridle, but they were scarcely worth the effort . . . old and battered. Besides, the same man who shot him also shot his horse. Shot them both through the head. It was good shooting. I went with my men where they found the bodies and stepped it off. From where the assassin kneeled to fire . . . and left his ejected carbine casing . . . to where the U.S. officer died, was two hundred yards, yet the man was hit in the head, then his horse was shot the same way, from the same distance. Very fine shooting."

"Yeah," agreed Claude, studying Fernando Bríon. "Did anyone down there backtrack the killer, or get a look at him, *señor*?"

"Well," replied Bríon in his careful English, "if

17

they did, Sheriff, they have been very careful not to say a word about it. You see, the place where the officer was killed, while it's on my land, it lies ten miles from my *hacienda* and it is so barren over there not even the cattle wander into that area very often."

"What the hell would Jonas Gantt be doing down there, then?" Claude asked, and the handsome, tall Mexican lifted his shoulders, dropped them, and wagged his head.

"Who knows, *señor*? There were no other tracks, but of course he'd been dead some time before anyone happened on to him. He'd been dried out by the sun . . . you understand?"

Claude understood. The same thing had happened to the one he'd had to bury. Just a bunch of angular bones fixed rigidly in place by a skin that had dried hard and dark, like old rawhide.

"Anyone else live thereabouts?" asked Rainey.

The Mexican's response didn't help at all. "No one, *señor*. I own all that desert down there. Not even Indians live on it. For one thing, there's no water. For another, no grass for horses, so there is no game for men . . . even *Indios* . . . to live off. No, *amigo*, I've gone over it all in my mind. It just makes no sense . . . unless your friend was on his way to some secret place, perhaps to meet another man, perhaps on a trail only he knew about."

18

Fernando Brìon stood up. Claude stirred himself to do likewise. He hadn't mentioned the bloodstained money and neither had the younger man. Brìon smiled. "You wonder why a Mexican takes the time to come up here and bring you these things along with the news of that man's death. Well, *amigo*, my father came from New York. His name was Bryan. In Mexico the nearest anyone can come to that is Brìon. You understand?"

Rainey understood. He thanked Brìon, shook his hand, and watched him head down toward the livery barn, on his way back to Mexico and his *hacienda*.

Rainey went inside, lit a lamp, examined the dead U.S. lawman's effects carefully, found nothing that would offer any kind of a key to the assassination, sighed mightily, and pushed the things aside to write another one of those letters that he afterward took to the stage office to be delivered at Phoenix, where the nearest U.S. marshal's office was.

Beyond that, he could only speculate, which is precisely what he did. Furthermore, since it was now definitely established that someone *did* know about the mummy he'd buried out on Boot Hill, that same someone undoubtedly had killed the U.S. marshal, which of course was too bad. But more to the immediate point, that same killer unquestionably knew about the $10,000.

19

Sheriff Rainey could see his dream of a fine white-painted schoolhouse for Springville slowly dissolving.

Even if he'd wanted to, which he had no desire to do particularly, he couldn't have kept the purpose of the handsome Mexican's visit to Springville a secret. Of course all the waning interest flared to life again. Wild rumors and even wilder speculations started up again. Barney Whitsun, who normally was shrewd and level-headed, wanted to know why Claude hadn't locked up this Fernando Bríon. When Claude irritably asked on what grounds, Barney had said on the grounds that he knew too damned much. Claude's reply to that had been blunt. "Then I'd have to lock up all the other folks around the country as well, you included Barney, for as I hear it, everyone knows a heap more about this mess than I do."

One week and one day later another stranger rode down Springville's wide and dusty main thoroughfare. Because folks were by this time keyed up to their limit, every man or woman who saw the stranger enter town from the west, powder-fine trail dust whitening his shoulders and hat, eyed him with quick, hard suspicion.

He was a heavy-boned youngish man who stood under six feet and had a face as dark as any Indian, from looking into the desert sun most of his life. He moved with a quiet confidence and his pale eyes, which contrasted sharply with the bronze of his skin, lent him a sinister appearance in the view of those who'd become almighty suspicious of any stranger.

His horse was leggy and deep-chested, a powerful chestnut gelding with dark mane and tail. It was a young horse full of vitality and honed-down stamina. In short, it was the kind of horse men rode who might have reason to run far and long on a moment's notice. That kind of an animal cost a great deal of money. Outlaws usually owned horses like that. Honest men could neither afford them, nor had much need for that much speed, stamina, and power.

It was a Saturday with most of the range riders and owners in town, when this new stranger rode in and put up his beast at the livery barn, and afterward beat off dust and drank beer up at the Oasis under the covertly appraising eyes and closed, suspicious faces of the local cowmen and townsmen.

The stranger, Jack Mather noticed, made a leisurely long study in his back-bar mirror of the saloon's patrons. He had to feel the suspicion, the antagonism, in the air, yet he stood there all loose and slouching, sipping his beer as relaxed as a man could be.

After he left the voices started. No one bothered to wander outside and see where he went from

21

Jack's place. Rumors began anew; he was the assassin; he'd come for the money in Barney's safe; he was a hired killer; Claude should lock him up at once.

But Claude didn't lock up the stranger. The idea never once crossed his mind, for the stranger's next stop after leaving Mather's place was Claude's office down at the jailhouse, where he showed Claude his badge and said his name was Arch Clayton, deputy U.S. marshal from the Raton, New Mexico, office. He'd been sent to Springville because there were no deputies available from the Phoenix office.

It all sounded perfectly sound and logical. Claude had brought forth Jonas Gantt's effects for Clayton to examine minutely, and Claude also told him about Fernando Bríon's visit. Beyond that he felt his way, giving all the details about the dead man he'd buried at Boot Hill, and minimizing the part about the bloodstained money. He couldn't of course just omit mentioning the money, but he didn't over-emphasize it, either.

Still, Arch Clayton said he wanted to see it, so Claude reluctantly took him over to Barney's general store office and showed it to him. The loafers outside at once figured out Clayton was another federal lawman, and spread out over town to pass this along. It didn't change anything; the rumormongers simply transposed the truth over the lies and went right on regarding Clayton with strong suspicion and distaste.

It was Newton Douglas, in town this same Saturday night with all his riders from the ranch, who made it a point to walk down to Rainey's office after supper and barge in upon the talk Claude and Clayton were having. He informed the lawmen what was being said. This annoyed Claude but it seemed to only amuse the deputy U.S. marshal. Clayton's pale eyes were droll as he said: "It's the same everywhere a deputy marshal shows up. There's just one bad feature to it. In large towns no one pays very much attention. In small places like Springville the talk gets back to the man or men. I'd just as soon have no notion there was another lawman around. Especially in cases like this one where the killer seems to be the bushwhacking type. I never grew an eye in the back of my head, and just about anyone can slip up behind a man two hundred yards away. If he's a good enough shot . . ."

Douglas gravely nodded, then he said: "Mister Clayton, everyone's been wondering. I reckon it's natural. But my particular question is . . . why, in over a month, hasn't someone tried to get hold of that ten thousand dollars?"

"That's the easy part," Clayton replied. "The first man to ride into Springville to prove he's got legitimate claim on that money will imme-diately have to explain away two murders. Not even a fortune such as this bloodstained ten thousand dollars is going to inspire very many men to stick their necks into that kind of a noose."

Douglas had evidently thought about this, too, because he spread out his hands and said deprecatingly: "Accusing a man of something and being able to hang him with proof, when as I understand it there've been no witnesses at all, are two different things."

Clayton's smile wavered slightly while he made a narrow study of Newton Douglas. "Under the law, Mister Douglas, neither your sheriff nor I have to let a suspect wander around until we can nail his hide to the wall. Suspicion of murder is a good enough charge to lock a man up and keep him locked up for a long while. That's the one element in crime folks generally don't understand . . . once you commit a crime, you can't undo it. You can't even change anything about it. But the law can dissect it over and over again, until something is found that'll eventually lead to an arrest."

Newt sat a while in deep thought, then departed, looking pensive. Clayton asked about him, and Claude told him all he had to know, which was enough, really, to allay the stranger's suspicions. Then Clayton said he'd be leaving Springville in the morning and Claude's eyes clouded.

"Gantt operated the same way," he said. "If you

go south of the border, someone'll eventually bring me back your gun and badge."

Clayton fished out the badge and tossed it upon Claude's desk. "Rule number one," he said. "Gantt overlooked it or just plain didn't care. Never go down into Mexico packing a U.S. lawman's badge." He stood up. He was a deceptively built man. Muscle was punched down hard under his skin. He didn't look it at first glance, but there wasn't an ounce of fat on Arch Clayton anywhere, and he weighed two hundred pounds despite the fact that he was only five feet and ten inches tall.

Claude, who'd made a lifelong study of men, recognized in this one all the attributes of the genuine killer. Not an assassin, or a professional gunfighter; those kinds came and went without living to get gray over the ears. But this kind of a man, who could kill equally as well with gun, knife, or fists, without giving that impression at all, was the real natural killer.

Claude escorted him out into the settling dusk and watched Clayton stride across to the hotel. He had a feeling that Arch Clayton would go down into Mexico and come back. He also had a feeling of quiet resignation; someone was going to end up getting that $10,000 after all. Claude's dream of a white-painted schoolhouse faded again, in his mind, as it had faded a time or two before. In irritation he growled at himself for ever entertaining such a grandiose idea. Springville didn't have but thirty or forty kids anyway, and that included the whole blessed countryside.

He turned, locked the jailhouse, and started up toward the Oasis, changed his mind across the road because he didn't feel like answering a hundred questions, and headed instead for his room, and bed, at the hotel.

Chapter Three

In due course, which was logical because the Registrar of Brands had a prosaic job and did everything in a properly prosaic manner, one of the stages brought a letter to Sheriff Rainey about the mark on the dead horse. It wasn't actually a registered brand, only the mark of a small horse raiser over by Raton used to identify his animals. There was of course no law as yet requiring all livestock markings to be registered, which the Registrar pointed out almost mournfully in his letter, therefore he couldn't do much more than give an outline of the brand, based upon little more than cursory information, frequently erroneous. But that horse rancher up near Raton specialized in steeldust cross animals. He had quality horses. The only ones he used his little mark upon were the best of his herds. And, oh, yes, his name was Archer Clayton.

Claude sat for a long time gazing at that letter. Something jangled discordantly in the back of his brain. Of course there was no law saying a deputy U.S. marshal couldn't also own a ranch and breed up fine quality horses. Pat Garrett, killer of Billy the Kid, had ranched on the side while he'd also been a peace officer.

But there seemed to Claude to be just too much

coincidence here. That dead man's horse had come from Clayton's herd, which meant also, in all probability, that both the man Claude had buried, as well as Clayton, came from the same area—Raton, which lay up against the mountains of New Mexico not very far south from Colorado's craggy uplands. Now Clayton shows up down at Springville, too, which was just about as far from the Raton country as a man could get, unless of course he went in the other direction and fetched up in Canada.

Claude decided to ride out and have another look at the mummified remains of that dead horse, and also to have another look around that sere, desolate cañon. He left town with the heat rolling in, passed at a slow gait downcountry to the east, and saw nothing but two dust devils whirling up out of Mexico until he got to the northerly rim of Dead Man's Cañon. But even then the sensation of being the only human being alive on earth persisted, for there was no movement, no sound, no brushy growth except only very occasionally, in all the world around him.

He descended uncomfortably into the wide, barren cañon. Heat lifted from the shimmering ground and piled up all around him. The air was sterile down here; it had scarcely enough oxygen. Claude's shirt darkened and his horse plodded along, glistening, until they came to the mummified remains of the horse.

The tunneling badgers had given up evidently because they'd gotten all the sustenance that could be gleaned. They'd heaved the carcass around apparently with little effort, for what had once been a thousand-pound horse was now little more than a brittle, brown envelope with some stiffly encased bones inside. One factor that helped, under the circumstances, was that mummified horses—or men for that matter—were practically scentless. There was no putrefaction; dehydration was too swift for the carcass to sour and rot as it would have done in damper or cooler country.

Claude dismounted, kicked the carcass over, and stood studying that place where the brand had been. The mark had been cut out—it was no longer there! Since Sheriff Rainey's last visit, someone had come up here and cut away the section of hide with a sharp knife; no other implement could have made the neat, square incision. Bone showed through and there were spider-web ligaments.

Claude turned slowly, gazing at the flinty earth. There were no tracks. But all that meant was that the man who'd removed the section of hide with the Clayton brand on it hadn't done so within the past day or two, for while it rarely rained in this desert country, hot winds sometimes blew up out of Mexico, off the shimmering Tamaulipas Plains, and filled the faint indentations with dust and sand. An Apache could have picked up the sign without doubt, but there hadn't been any Apaches down here—at least that anyone ever saw—in many years.

Claude stood hip-shot in the shade of his drooping mount and rolled a smoke. Clayton could have done it; at least he'd been somewhere close by when that section of hide had been carved out. Of course it could just as easily have been some damned curio seeker, too, or perhaps *Señor* Brion himself, although that didn't make a whole lot of sense to Claude as he stood and smoked and puzzled the thing over until the faint and distant whiplash sound of a gunshot brought him crashing back to the present.

His horse gave a little jump and switched its tail but Claude didn't see where the bullet struck. It wouldn't have kicked up enough dust in this dead, gravelly world anyway. Claude went to the horse, stepped up, and reined back a hundred or so feet before he paused, looking all around. His first calm thought was that either this wasn't the marksman who'd done the other killing here— and probably the Gantt killing down in Mexico, too—or else he was off his feed, because he'd missed clean.

His second thought was that, since he knew this country as well as any man alive, he just might be able to catch a glimpse of his private bush-whacker.

He reined up along the heat-blurred slope that he'd descended about a half hour earlier, paused to rest his mount on the rim, then dropped far enough northward to be out of sight of anyone down below in Dead Man's Cañon, and rode straight southward in the direction of the international line.

Where the higher desert began to slope downward and on ahead in the distant blue-blurred reaches he could make out the endless expanse of the Tamaulipas Plains over the border in Mexico. He searched hard for sign of a horseman, and found none at all. In every direction the land was as empty as the surface of the moon. He rode slowly and carefully, staying well away from the occasional little arroyos that splayed out like fingers, east and west. If that rifleman didn't have wings, he'd have to be down here somewhere. The view was uninterrupted in every direction. Since Claude couldn't see him, he was probably crouching in one of the little finger-like gullies.

There was a way to determine that and Claude set about doing it. After all, a man didn't follow the lawman's trade for nearly forty years without ending up under a plank, and fail to learn a few worthwhile tricks. He looked around, then headed for the nearest lift in the land. He'd be in perfect view up there, an ideal stationary target except that he picked a place which was well beyond gun range of even the closest arroyo, and there he dismounted, got into the shadow of his horse to make the ambusher's target even less inviting, then he squatted down and became simply another layer of the horse shadow.

For twenty minutes he squatted like that, until his horse got impatient and stamped a couple of times, but he still saw nothing. He commanded a decent view down into every blessed arroyo and cañon for several miles, and saw nothing, only the same tawny red-brown earth with its infrequent little stunted sedge bush no more than a foot high, and occasionally a lizard or horned toad or hairy spider, which went to make up the life and substance of this dead world.

Finally, with the heat sucking sweat off his hide before it even got to his shirt, Claude stood up resignedly, got back on his horse and debated whether to turn back or go on. He went on. He had two-thirds of the day left to squander and he was very curious. In the old days an Apache could have blended into the landscape like this, but only a very experienced Apache. Nowadays there weren't even any Indians left who could do what this bushwhacker had just done—dissolve into thin air in a place where there wasn't a decent hiding place in any direction.

The trick, of course, was to stay well out in the open as he rode southward, and to get the hell out of this country before dusk settled. He knew if his enemy was still around—and he felt certain that this one was handy at disappearing in the evening shadows—he could raise up off the earth and shoot a man out of his saddle at less than ten feet. That, too, had been one of the old-time Apache tricks.

Claude rolled a pebble under his tongue, tilted his hat brim forward, and rode straight down the gentle slope until he ran out of uphill country. He was then at the mouth of Dead Man's Cañon. If his enemy was anywhere close by, he'd have to be either back up the cañon in hiding—although only the Lord knew where—or else he'd have to be down across the line into Mexico, and Claude knew for a damned fact he hadn't gotten away in that direction because he'd squatted up there for twenty minutes watching for just such movement.

It never once occurred to him, for understandable reasons, that the ambusher might've skirted along under the base of the same hill Claude had ridden up and over, heading *westward,* not southward, in the direction of Springville, until he decided to ride up the middle of the broad, desolate cañon and see if he couldn't find the place from which the would-be assassin had fired at him.

He found the place. It was within five yards of where that earlier killer had kneeled and fired to kill the mysterious stranger Claude had buried. The ejected brass cartridge caught his eye while he was still three hundred feet distant. Sunlight glittered off that tubular object with all the evil intensity of death itself. He got down, carefully circled the area before picking up the spent casing, and had his answer. The bushwhacker hadn't run for Mexico at all; he'd headed straight back toward Springville. Claude swore long and loud, got fiercely back astride, and started toward Springville, too, picking up the other man's tracks now and then as he rode.

It was well into the afternoon before he arrived back in town. He went immediately to the livery barn to look over all the horses. A person didn't ride that long and hard under a midsummer desert sun and not sweat hell out of his horse. Even if he curried the animal, he couldn't hide the shrunken gut dehydration caused.

But there wasn't a tucked up horse either in the stalls or out back in the corrals. When the liveryman sauntered out mopping his face with a red bandanna to inquire what Rainey might be looking for, Claude only growled at him and went out into the roadway to begin a slow and meticulous stroll up one side of the road and down the other, looking at the tethered horses.

He found nothing there, either, so he strolled into the Oasis for a beer, and found no strangers there at all. It was more than just frustrating; it could also be dangerous. If all that bushwhacker'd had in mind was scaring Claude off, then he probably felt he'd made his point. But if there was something personal to this, then, since a man only had one life, Claude had to locate his particular enemy before he was himself located.

Jack Mather mentioned that Claude looked as though he'd been out in the heat of the day. Rainey acknowledged that he had, and asked if there were any strangers in town. Jack rolled his dark eyes. "Ain't two enough?" he asked. "By the way, have you heard from that second deputy marshal? I'd give odds they nail him down there, too, if you was of a mind, Claude."

"What kind of betting is that," growled Rainey. "You ought to be ashamed of yourself."

Mather went after a glass of beer for himself and returned with another one for Claude. He said: "It's not that I'm hoping anything happens to the second one, Claude. It's just that sometimes a feller has to break the monotony, and this way maybe he can pick up a dollar or two at the same time."

"Oh, sure," grumbled Claude, draining the last of his first glass and reaching for the second one. "Anyone come in here in the last hour or two who looked like he'd been riding hard or lying in some dust?"

Mather's dark eyes grew very still. Then he shook his head. "What's on your mind, Claude, what're you up to? Does it have to do with the ten thousand dollars?"

"Does asking tomfool questions break the

monotony, too?" countered the lawman, belching aside and afterward dragging the back of a scarred, hairy hand across wet lips. "Jack, I've had a bad feeling about that damned money ever since I put it in Barney's safe."

"Nothing's happened, except a couple of federal deputies come along, and they didn't stay around."

"I know. But that feeling I've had is getting worse."

"How about some bicarbonate of soda. You been eating in those greaser cafés again, Claude?"

Rainey finished the second beer, slapped down a coin, glared, and walked out of the saloon. Mather scooped up the coin, shrugged, and reached for his bar rag. It was evening finally, trade would shortly pick up, and best of all the heat would start to lessen.

Sheriff Rainey went down to his office and wrote a letter to the authorities up at Raton, New Mexico, asking a number of questions concerning a man named Arch Clayton. He also gave a general description—which was all he could give—of the mummified dead man riding the Clayton horse, described the animal also, and asked for information about him, too. Finally, he directed a letter to the U.S. marshal over at Phoenix asking two questions: One, was there a field office at Raton? Two, if there was such an office, did a deputy named Arch Clayton work out of it?

He then took these letters up to the stage office and afterward went to the pool hall, which lay south of Hank Smith's shoeing shop, and ate at the free lunch counter, played two rounds of snooker with a couple of Hightower cowboys he met up there, and then headed for his room at the hotel—euphemistically called a hotel while in reality it was a rooming house.

Lying in bed with the roadside window open, the late night sounds drifting up, he wrestled with the interlude of the strange gunshot. Why in tarnation had that damned idiot shot at him down there by the dead horse, and how did he come—whoever he was—to dust it for town instead of back down into Mexico where he had undoubtedly come from? Finally, and most annoying of all, how had that assassin managed to fade out in Springville like he had?

Chapter Four

It's never the answers that bother a man very much, it's the questions. Claude went about for the next two days with his eyes narrowed and wary. At the end of two days, however, he began to feel that his bushwhacker out there hadn't come into Springville to shoot him after all, or else he'd have tried it long before now.

That, of course, was the answer, and it relieved him in a sense. But the questions were piling up, and they continued to bother him right up until, after supper over at the jailhouse, Archer Clayton walked in out of the bland, hot night, as though he'd only been away an hour or two. He nodded and tossed his hat upon a bench, sank into a chair, and said it was almighty damned hot, riding the desert this time of year. He didn't even say hello or how are you or, has anything happened in Springville since I left.

Claude sat stonily studying the younger, heavier man. Eventually, playing his cards close, he said—"Nothing ever happens in the Springville country."—with enough sarcasm behind the words to make Clayton lift tired eyes. "Only, someone took a shot at me the other day out where that other fellow got killed."

Clayton's expression changed. "Oh, that," he

said carelessly. "That was me did that, Sheriff."

Claude's tough gaze narrowed a little more. "You? You're the one took that shot at me?"

Clayton nodded.

"Mind telling me why?"

"Because if I hadn't, they'd have killed you. I aimed close enough at your horse to make him jump. I didn't really aim at you at all."

"*They'd* have killed me?"

"You saw where a brand had been cut off that carcass out there?" asked Clayton, looking directly at Claude. "Well, they took care of that right after someone down in the Mex town of Rosario recognized me, tried a bushwhack that didn't come off, then came up here to hack off that brand. You see, Sheriff, the brand on that horse was my mark."

Claude pulled back into himself until he had a double chin. He was suspicious, wary, and perplexed. Also, he was beginning to think Archer Clayton was too glib with his answers. "Go on," he said non-committally. "Keep talking."

"I reckon I'd better go back and start at the beginning."

"That might help," said Claude, mildly sarcastic.

"The fellow you found dead out there with his horse . . . and buried out in your Boot Hill cemetery . . . was my partner. He owned some land that adjoined my ranch up near Raton, over in New Mexico."

"Yes," murmured old Claude, still sternly drawing away.

"He and I found an old cache of Spanish gold. We sold some of it to a trader from over around Socorro, and he re-sold the old gold coins to a big *hacendado* down Mexico way."

"Name of Brion?" asked Claude softly.

Clayton, in the midst of speaking, looked sharply at Sheriff Rainey with his mouth still open. Gradually he closed it. "You fool a man, Sheriff," he murmured. "You surely do. So you figured it out, did you?"

"Nope. Brion's the Mexican I told you about who brought Jonas Gantt's stuff back here and gave it to me."

Clayton digested that for a while. Eventually he said: "I reckon it was just an oversight, Sheriff, you referring to that Mexican simply as such, instead of naming him." Clayton was gazing straight at Rainey when he said this, as though Claude's answer would have weight with his judgment of Rainey, one way or another.

"There are thousands of Mexicans in this border country, Mister Clayton. Even fancy ones like this Brion are still only Mexes. If you'd hung around a day or two when you came by before, it would've come out. I sure never attached much importance to his name. Just a taller than average, nice-looking Mex *hacendado* . . . rancher."

"All right," Clayton murmured, revealing nothing of his inner judgment the way he said it. Then he turned back to what they'd been discussing. "Brion bought those old Spanish coins. Then he sent word, if my partner or I'd bring down some more to his place in Mexico, he'd buy them direct and no one'd have to pay the Socorro trader."

"So your partner went."

"That's right. And Brion bought the coins." Clayton fished out his makings and began manufacturing a cigarette. "This much I know for fact. From here on I'm guessing. But Brion showed me the coins he'd bought, day before yesterday at his ranch."

"Wait a minute," broke in Claude skeptically. "How could you tell one old Spanish coin from another, Mister Clayton?"

"I'm coming to that, Sheriff. Don't get impatient. Anyway, Brion showed me the coins. They were the same ones my partner took down to sell him. Brion said he'd paid my partner ten thousand U.S. dollars in paper bills, and my pardner left with the money in a small wooden box."

"Here goes my schoolhouse," murmured Claude, and Clayton looked inquiringly at him as he struck the match for his smoke. "Nothing," said Claude, in a louder voice. "Nothing at all, Mister Clayton. Let's have the rest of it."

41

"You know the rest of it, Sheriff, except for one small thing. My partner was waylaid by some Mexican ambushers who tried to kill him for the ten thousand dollars. They almost succeeded, but he shot two of them and the other three fled. One of the men he shot got the little box and was trying to run with it when my partner killed him."

"Is that how you figure the blood got on the money?"

Clayton nodded, trickling smoke from his nostrils and narrowly eyeing Rainey. "It's the only way it could've happened, since my partner wasn't wounded in the fight."

"Well, now, Mister Clayton, since you never talked to your partner after he left Raton, heading for Mexico, how do you know any of this happened?"

Clayton smoked a moment, still narrowly eyeing Sheriff Rainey, then he stood up. "If you've got a minute to spare, I'd be glad to show you my proof."

Claude also stood up. "I've got all the time in the world," he said, and followed Clayton out of the office, down the roadway toward the southern end of town where some abandoned adobe *jacales* stood, and stopped only when Clayton killed his smoke underfoot, stepped through a doorless opening into the rank, dark interior of one of the little hovels, and beckoned Rainey inside, too.

Claude stepped carefully to the doorway and

looked in. He was being prudent about all this; he had no reason to act otherwise, which Clayton seemed to appreciate, so he crossed the room, struck a match, and held it above a bundle of rags with a man inside them, lying apparently lifeless upon the earthen floor. Claude's breath caught in his throat. He craned ahead as Clayton's match flared then went out.

"Who is that?" he demanded softly.

"A Mexican brigand," replied Clayton, digging for another match. "Come on in, Sheriff. He isn't here for long."

Finally, Claude stepped through the doorway, looked quickly left and right, then stepped up beside the younger man and looked down. The Mexican had been shot. He very clearly was dying. Claude asked a question: "You do this to him?"

Clayton nodded and kneeled down. In smooth Spanish he asked the dying Mexican if he rode for Fernando Brion. Claude had to lean over to catch the soft-sighed reply.

"*Sí.*"

"And you were one of the *buscaderos Señor* Brion sent to kill the *gringo* with the wooden box?"

"*Sí, señor. . . .*"

Clayton looked around. "You understand Spanish?" he asked. Claude nodded and asked the dying man a question of his own.

"How did you get shot, *amigo*?"

In faint, wavering words, the dying brigand said he'd also been sent to ambush this other *yanqui*, but this one, too, was of the devil's own breed of men. He'd routed the four bushwhackers and had shot the dying man. Then, when Clayton started to speak, Claude motioned for silence while he asked his last question of the dying man.

"*Paisano*, who killed the other *gringo* . . . the one with the lawman's badge in his pocket?"

The Mexican tried to focus his eyes upon his interrogator, but they only rolled aimlessly from side to side as he answered. "It was done by order of *Don* Fernando, when the *vaqueros* found that one on the trail of the men who finally killed the *gringo* carrying the wooden box up over the line, *señor*. . . ."

Claude straightened up. He glanced at Clayton, who was watching him, then made a little useless gesture. "Maybe if we got this man to the doctor he'd . . . ?"

Claude didn't finish it and Arch Clayton made no attempt to answer it as he uncoiled and stood up straight. No one, very obviously, was going to save this dying man. The most merciful thing that could be done for him would be to leave him in peace and quiet, and dark coolness.

Claude returned to the sunshine and waited. Clayton came out moments later. He had an empty bottle of whiskey in one hand. As Claude looked,

Clayton said: "I'll get another bottle. That's how I kept him going the last couple of days. It won't cure him . . . nothing can do that . . . but it'll make going out a lot easier for him."

"You brought him back with you . . . in that shape?" Claude was incredulous.

Clayton shrugged. "He's tough. They're all tough, Sheriff. I wanted him to be able to talk when you saw him. The hardest part was riding double. My horse is a stout one, but still and all it's a bad time of year under the best circumstances. On top of that we had to make a sashay over toward that cañon. The Mexican told me he'd been sent up to cut out the brand on my partner's dead horse. I wanted to test that, to see whether he'd lied or not. That's when I saw them stalking you around the southerly end of the cañon out there. They were going to drop you just like they dropped my partner, and in the same damned place. So, I shot at you myself, to warn you, then I had to ride like hell to get up here to Springville before you . . . or they . . . got around to where I was, and got me first."

Claude moved over against the front of the *jacal* and leaned there. He was getting his answers now, all right, but they seemed only to pose more troublesome questions. "Who are they?" he asked.

"Bríon's guerillas. His *vaquero pistoleros.* He's got a small army of them down on his ranch.

45

You know how those Mex *hacendados* operate, Sheriff. When there are no revolutions going on, they work their herds of cattle. The *vaqueros* in both cases are their soldiers or their cowboys, but they obey. Believe me, Sheriff, they obey." Clayton jerked a thumb over his shoulder toward the interior of the adobe hovel, his meaning amply clear. "One more question," said Claude, narrowing his eyes against the sun smash. "Why? Why all this killing?"

"The Spanish coins, Sheriff. Now I'll tell you about them, too. These aren't just any old Spanish doubloons. They are made like every other Spanish gold sovereign, but each one of them has a mark scratched upon it so small you have to look to find it with a magnifying glass."

"Mint symbol?" asked Claude, not quite comprehending.

"Nope. Each of those coins has a different mark. My partner and I recorded each one in a little book before we sold the coins. My partner never knew what those marks signified. Neither did the trader down at Socorro, but Fernando Brión knew. Whoever gets all those coins has to put all the little scratches together, Sheriff, like he's making a map, then he'll have the map, for that's exactly what it is, a map to a very old hidden cache of Spanish gold bars and more coins."

Claude gazed for a long moment at the younger man. He asked an irrelevant question. "Mister, where did you get that deputy U.S. marshal's badge you left with me before you went down into Mexico?"

For a second or two Clayton seemed off balance, then he said, giving his head a wag: "Sheriff, that ten thousand dollars over in the safe at the general store is only a small part of what that old cache will bring. And you're interested in a two-bit badge."

"Son," Claude said crisply, "when a man gets to be my age all the damned gold the old Spaniards sweated out of the Indians in this whole blessed hemisphere doesn't mean as much to him as one good human life. Where did you get that badge?"

"From the resident deputy U.S. marshal at Raton. He swore me in when I told him I was going down to look for my partner, who was long overdue getting back home."

Claude didn't exactly care whether that was the truth or not. He only wanted to force Clayton into telling him something, just anything, so that when his reply came back from the marshal's office over at Phoenix, he'd have an answer to the main thing, and that was, simply, whether Archer Clayton was a liar or not.

According to Claude Rainey's view of men, if they lied at all, he wanted nothing to do with them. All he wanted to know now was whether he dared put any credence in *anything* Archer Clayton had told him.

47

A little noise came from inside the *jacal*. Clayton turned and disappeared inside for a moment. Claude heard his voice low and soft, speaking swift Spanish. Then there was silence. Claude dug out his makings and started to work on a smoke he felt no desire for at all. What a lousy way for a man to die, even a murderer and bushwhacker like that Mexican brigand obviously was, on a dirt floor in an abandoned mud hovel, in the dark.

He lit up, exhaled, and waited a moment or two longer before starting back uptown toward his jailhouse. On the way he made up his mind about two things. He wasn't going to believe or disbelieve a single thing Clayton had told him until he got back replies to those letters he'd sent off earlier, and he wasn't going to turn his back on Archer Clayton, either.

On just one score was he perfectly satisfied. His initial assessment of Clayton had been a bull's-eye. Clayton was a dangerous man, a genuine killer. The question was did Clayton kill legally or illegally? That was exactly what Claude made up his mind to determine, and soon, too.

Chapter Five

Archer Clayton didn't appear again at the jailhouse until well after dark. Claude didn't worry. He thought he knew what Clayton was up to, so he went over to the café for supper, had a glass of ale up at Mather's saloon, then made a round of town before heading on back.

Clayton was waiting for him on the bench outside the jailhouse. He sat down gravely and they talked. Rainey's first question took care of the immediate past.

"You been burying him?"

Clayton said: "And this time of year it's damned hard digging."

So that settled that; the Mexican bushwhacker was dead. Claude then said: "I reckon I'd better alert the town vigilance committee. Just in case Bríon rounds up a herd of those other cowboys of his and tries hitting the town for that ten thousand dollars. He knows it's here."

Clayton looked pained. In a tone of voice he might have used toward a child he said: "Sheriff, Fernando Bríon doesn't give a tinker's damn about that ten thousand dollars. It didn't mean anything to him when he handed it over to my partner. What Bríon wants is the rest of those gold coins. And I'm the only one who can tell him

49

where they are." Clayton waited until an elderly couple strolled by in the warm night, then said: "If he finds the cache of gold by putting all the little scratches together off those coins, he'll probably have so much more wealth than my ten thousand dollars over there in the storekeeper's safe, it'll look like chicken feed to him."

Claude nodded. He understood that part well enough, it was simply that he couldn't altogether give up the notion that he was protecting that $10,000 against anyone, legal or illegal, who'd come for it. As Al Trail, Hightower ranch's range boss, had said, sooner or later someone was going to come for that money. Well, as it turned out, it looked as though Al had been only partly right. It looked like someone *had* come for it all right, but he didn't really care as much about the $10,000 as he cared about other things.

Claude said: "Mister Clayton, why don't you just sell those damned gold coins to Brion? You've already copied down all the telltale marks. You can put them together into the map and get to that cache before Brion can."

"I've thought of that, Sheriff, and I've also thought of altering a few of the little marks, or of keeping back five or six of the key coins, just to bait Brion up over the line where I can settle with him for what he has done to my partner."

"Well . . . ?"

Clayton shook his head. "I want more than just

revenge, Sheriff. I want to bust Fernando Bríon down into the dust. I aim to destroy him completely, and that also goes for his assassins. But first I want the name of the one who killed my partner, and the name of the one who killed that U.S. deputy marshal."

"It looks to me, Mister Clayton, that when you find out the names, it's going to turn out to be the same man," said Rainey. "I can give you a pretty good idea of how to determine which of Bríon's cowboys he is. Just bait a trap at long range and see which one of those Mexicans steps up to try his aim at a couple of hundred yards."

Clayton said no more about this, so evidently the same idea had crossed his mind earlier. "Sheriff, Bríon knows by now I got his bushwhacker. It'll only take him a second or two to figure out why I took that dead Mexican with me . . . to sweat some answers out of him."

Claude, listening closely, began to get the gist of Clayton's thoughts. They brought him up straight on the bench. The implications suddenly had Claude Rainey right in the middle of what could very soon become a savagely bloody encounter.

"As soon as Bríon knows I'm on to him," went on Clayton, "he's going to send those killers of his up here, sure as shooting. It won't be a matter of killing me if they can help it. It'll be a matter of catching me alone, getting me away some place where they can build their torture fire and strip off my boots and socks. You understand?"

Claude said, brushing aside the last question: "Get on that chestnut horse, Mister Clayton, and head out of Springville as fast as he can leg it."

The younger man cast a sidelong glance at Sheriff Rainey, his eyes sardonic. "Go where, Sheriff? Back up to Raton? I'd never make it. But even if I did . . . then what? They'd come up there, too. No, I'll stay right here. One place is as good as any other."

Claude nodded. "I was afraid you'd feel that way." He sighed. "You're dragging me and my town into this with you."

Clayton shrugged. That didn't seem to worry him. "If not you and your town, Sheriff, then some other sheriff and some other town." He stood up. "I need a drink, care to join me?"

They went along together, walking slowly and thoughtfully up toward Mather's bar, which was northward and across the road. Springville was lively around them as the night deepened. That little sickle moon up there had thickened at the girth, fleshed out a little at both upper and lower horns, and now was casting downward some genuine brightness. As Sheriff Rainey walked along in deep thought, it occurred to him that if those *vaqueros* who'd been on the verge of shooting him down at Dead Man's Cañon were still north of the border, they might very probably be skulking around on the outskirts of Springville right this minute, seeking Arch Clayton. It also occurred to him that Brion's visit to Springville returning the effects of Jonas Gantt hadn't been at all as generously philanthropic as it had seemed at the time. Brion had obviously come to town for a look at the place, at the people, even at the variety of law enforcement that existed.

Claude paused to say: "Mister Clayton, you said you'd already worked up a map off those coins, didn't you?"

"Yeah. I've got it in a little book."

"In a little book," murmured Claude, raising shrewdly appraising eyes. "And this little book . . . you've got it on you right now?"

"Yes," replied the younger man, stopping to turn and gaze at Rainey.

"That's what I was afraid of," Claude murmured, and resumed walking. "I'm also afraid of something else, Mister Clayton."

"That Brion'll hit your town with his *vaqueros* looking for me, Sheriff?"

"No, not exactly that, Mister Clayton. I'm afraid the reason you're carrying that little book with you, down here, is because this is where that damned map told you the rest of the bullion is buried."

Clayton's eyes widened slightly as he paced along, gazing at Sheriff Rainey. "I said it before, Sheriff, but I'll say it again . . . you sure fool a man."

Claude brushed what definitely was a compliment aside and raised his bushy brows. "Well . . . ?" he asked.

"You're dead right, Sheriff."

"Yeah. I'd rather just be right, though. Now I do need that drink."

They reached the Oasis and barged on in. It was a mid-week night with a few card games going at the tables, and with a handful of range men up along the bar, but mostly the patrons this night were townsmen. Barney Whitsun was there, along with Hank Smith, the blacksmith, and a few other local merchants or tradesmen. Jack Mather came down to them for their order, looking bored. Clayton called for whiskey and Mather looked at him with rising interest. Around the room elsewhere other men looked up, also recognizing Clayton as the second of those two deputy U.S. marshals. They showed the same astonishment at seeing Clayton alive that Mather showed. After Jack had gone for their drinks, Sheriff Rainey said from the edge of his mouth: "They didn't expect to see you come back all in one piece and standing up." He said no more until the drinks came, and Jack had gone back down his bar in response to a cowboy's call. Then he said: "Mister Clayton, if these men knew what you'd brought back with you, I've got a hunch they'd pick you up bodily, tie you on your horse, and hooraw you out of Springville."

54

The younger man was skeptical. "You could always tell them," he said, tipping back his head and dropping the shot of whiskey straight down. Then he pushed the glass away, twisted to lean upon the bar, and said: "Of course that wouldn't make much difference, Sheriff, because those first ten coins we sold to Brion were the ones with the first few miles of the journey scratched on them."

Claude's eyes rolled. "Wait a minute," he whispered. "Are you saying they'd lead him to Springville?"

"Dead right, Sheriff."

"I wish you'd quit using that expression."

"Excuse me, Sheriff. The answer is . . . you are perfectly correct. They'd bring Fernando Brion right into the heart of your town, down near the southern end where those ancient Mexican *jacales* are."

Claude signaled for two more drinks and hooked his elbows over the bar, looking morosely at his own worried, seamed, and leathery countenance in Jack's back-bar mirror. Above the mirror hung an old painting of a Spanish *conquistador* in full armor, on a snorting horse. The Lord knew where Mather had ever come across that dark and sinister old work of art, and it was out of place in its crude frontier barroom setting, but evidently Jack had liked the thing, so there it hung.

Sheriff Rainey raised his second glass in a little salute to the hawk-nosed armored Spaniard and said under his breath—"Here's to you . . . you damned louse."—and drank his whiskey off neat, put the glass down, and turned to see Clayton's eyes looking at him in wry amusement. "What's so funny?" he demanded.

"You, Sheriff, and that painting up there. What did you expect them to do when they conquered the Indians around here a couple of hundred years back, sit down and raise kids and corn and squash?"

"No," stated Rainey. "But if they'd taken their lousy gold with 'em when they left, I'd've thought a heap more of them."

"Bríon wouldn't've, Sheriff. Care for another drink?"

"Two's my limit. You staying at the hotel?"

"Tonight I will, yes. But first I'll go see to my horse. Meet you at the rooming house in a little while."

Rainey watched Clayton depart, was still staring over at the roadside doors through which he'd vanished when Jack Mather walked up and said: "Claude, that one must be tougher'n a boiled owl. I'd sure have lost money on him, wouldn't I?"

"Maybe," muttered Claude. "But his little chore is a long way from being finished, so you might still be right." With that enigmatic remark, Sheriff Rainey also walked out of the saloon.

Down at the rooming house he routed out the landlord, paid for another room, took the key, and went down into the tiny lobby to sit and wait, so Clayton would know which room was his when he returned.

He didn't return.

Claude Rainey was comfortable in the one old overstuffed chair in the lobby, and fell sound asleep there. When he awakened, there was that little pre-dawn chill to the air. He sat a moment, drawing together all the interrupted threads of thought, then stiffly arose, gingerly arched his back to rid himself of a kink, scratched his head, and walked outside. Springville was as quiet and still and unlighted as a graveyard. He went southward to the first intersecting roadway and craned around toward the horizon. It was at least 5:00 in the morning. That had a very sobering effect.

He walked on down to the livery barn, kicked the chair leg of the drowsing night hawk until the man came awake, then asked if the hostler had seen a husky man on a handsome big breedy chestnut horse ride out of town. The night hawk not only hadn't seen such a man ride out of town, he hadn't seen *anyone* ride out of town.

It was pointless to ask if Clayton had kept his chestnut at the barn, but Claude asked anyway. He drew exactly the reply he'd expected.

"No. Ain't had no such a horse as you describe at all, Sheriff."

Claude eased off the little tie-down thong holding his six-gun in its holster and went over among the eerie, dark, and utterly hushed mud hovels at the lower end of town. He went through them one at a time, and since none of them had more than two rooms, he didn't have any difficulty determining that neither Arch Clayton nor his chestnut horse were in any of them. He did, however, find in one *jacal* indications where someone'd very recently kept a horse. This house was directly across a crooked little alleyway from where Brion's dead Mexican had cashed in the afternoon before.

With little hope of success Sheriff Rainey completed his search and emerged back upon the main roadway just as the sun began climbing from over the edge of the eastern horizon, sending up lovely pink streamers of soft light in advance of its full rising.

Claude stood and rubbed his beard-stubbled chin. He had a very strong idea of what had happened and it frightened him. When a man has lived among Mexicans long enough, he makes a rather basic discovery; while these people are the most hospitable, courteous, generous, and friendly people under the sun, they also have an inherent and off-handed cruelty that is also second to none under the sun.

Brion would know all the methods. He'd have learned them from his *peones*, who had in turn learned many of them from Apache Indians, or from other *peones* who'd heard of the tortures

58

employed by the old-time Spaniards. Burning the bottom of the feet was only the first and gentlest of the tortures used.

Claude went over to his jailhouse, got his booted carbine, shoved an extra box of cartridges into his pocket, and went down to the livery barn calling for his horse to be saddled at once. While he stood waiting, he wondered about routing out a few townsmen such as tough and scarred Jack Mather and the blacksmith, Hank Smith, to go along with him. What prevented him from doing this was the alacrity with which his horse was brought forth, saddled and bridled, as well as the knowledge that he'd have to kill another half hour or so waiting for them to get dressed, rigged out, and ready to ride.

He mounted and buckled in the saddle boot, then drifted on outside of town, beginning to ride in a big circle. It was too early for interlopers to have marred Brion's fresh tracks; he was counting very heavily on that, for otherwise he'd have no idea in which direction to look.

Dawn light steadily brightened, and that helped, too. When he found the tracks, finally, they went southeast.

Chapter Six

For a while it looked as though the tracks might head straight for the border, and that was what made Sheriff Rainey a little desperate, for if they did head down that way, and made no stop between Springville and the boundary line, then no matter how far or hard Claude rode, he was going to be much too late. The Mexicans had a good two-hour start on him, and perhaps even a three-hour start.

But the tracks veered off, eventually, heading over toward the empty, eerie desolation of Dead Man's Cañon. Claude was relieved. He was also puzzled. What was the point in Brión or his *majordomo*—his range boss—whichever was doing all this, in taking Archer Clayton over to where his partner had died?

Also, Claude worried about something else, something infinitely more immediate to his own well-being. Clayton's abductors had utilized the darkness of full night to make their grab and subsequent run. Claude was crossing a barren, empty world out in plain sight, alone, in the first soft blush of new daylight. Brión's men would have spies out watching their back trail. They'd see Claude coming, and, if they were worth their Mexican salt, they'd drop down in a gulch somewhere and wait to pick him off as he drifted past.

To avoid at least the last part of this, Claude did as he'd done before—he rode well away from any logical places for assassins to hide. Also, he left the tracks when he was satisfied where they were taking him, cut far around to the west, then the north, and emerged upon the high plateau above the cañon, up where he'd squatted that other time when he'd been in trouble out here.

This way he couldn't be ambushed. They'd probably spot him eventually, but at least he'd also see them before they could get close enough to open up.

He made a smoke in early morning coolness and edged over as far as he dared to go on horseback toward the northerly slope. That permitted him a fairly good view down into the broad, barren cañon. From there he went along on foot, crouched over and with his carbine in one fist, like an Apache the way he trotted closer to the downhill slope. Finally, because he could see nearly all the cañon below except that spot where the mummified remains of the horse lay, anyone down below, if they raised their eyes, would also be able to see him. So Claude got down on all fours and crawled the last hundred and fifty feet.

Then he saw them, and obviously they'd been there an hour or two. Their horses were standing ground-hitched and drowsy a short distance from the mummified remains of the horse. There were four of the Mexicans, three with bullet-studded bandoleers slung cross-ways over their chests, while the fourth one, taller, blacker, more fiercely mustached than his *vaquero* companions, wore his six-gun tied to the leg and hung low like any other border gunfighter. Also, this one didn't wear the enormous sombrero of the Mexicans with him; he wore instead a typical Southwestern range man's hat with a brim only four or five inches wide.

On the ground, sitting with his arms lashed behind his back, was Archer Clayton. Standing with the other horses was Clayton's powerful and breedy big chestnut horse. From time to time one of the three *peones* would turn and covetously gaze out where the chestnut stood. If they said anything among themselves, Claude couldn't hear it, or, for that matter, even see their lips move, but he didn't have to; he knew that look on the face of lifelong horsemen. It was the same look men elsewhere put upon handsome, voluptuous, very desirable women.

Claude belly-crawled as far as two little side-by-side bitterbrush bushes, stunted until they didn't stand a full eighteen inches off the flinty ground. He kept his carbine back. There was ample sun-light to make a twinkling reflection.

That big Mexican reached, hauled Clayton to his feet with one hand, slapped him viciously across the face with his free hand, and let Clayton go. He fell and rolled, trying dazedly to sit up again. The Mexican called him something in a fiercely loud voice. Claude heard that, although he couldn't distinguish the words.

Evidently the physical beating wasn't over yet, which meant the Mexicans didn't have to start gathering twigs for their torture fire. The three *peones* lounged indifferently while their *jefe*—chief—continued to work on Clayton. The big Mexican leaned, raised Clayton again, held him with one hand, and pulled a big-bladed, wickedly shining knife. He flourished the knife for emphasis, then bent his head close and said something. Clayton was stiffly straining against the little grass rope—called a *mecate* by Mexicans, McCarty by American cowboys—twisting and bunching his powerful shoulders. He could guess what was coming. First, the nostrils were slit, then the ears were punctured, then the eyelids were fleshed away. But these were only the preliminaries.

Claude sighed, wet a finger, held it aloft to catch the direction of the moving air, pushed his carbine gingerly through between the pair of little bushes, clamped his hat lower until it was fully down in front of his eyes, then he settled comfortably in the gritty dust and curled up around his carbine. The range was considerably farther than most men who used carbines with their short barrels rather than long-barreled rifles were accustomed to. At least the sun was just beginning to turn brightly brittle and fiercely hot, so there was as yet no shimmering blur to mar his sighting.

He waited, taking down big gulps of air and letting them out slowly again, his slitted eyes fixed with deadly intensity on the big Mexican's thick chest. He couldn't fire as long as Clayton was that close. He'd have to wait until the Mexican either knocked Clayton down again, or slashed him and Clayton recoiled from the pain.

Those three loafing *peones* down there were finally taking an interest. They sat down, carbines across their laps, silently watching. Claude shot them one glance, then after that completely ignored them. His palms got oily so he wiped them on his shirt front and resumed his firing position again, swearing under his breath because the Mexican was haranguing Clayton instead of striking him. Then he struck, using the heavy handle of his big knife. Clayton's knees turned rubbery but he refused to go down. The Mexican stepped back, roared a violent curse, and struck again. That time Clayton went down.

Claude fired.

The sound was a thin, high, twig-snapping sound in the immensity of all that emptiness. It didn't even make an echo. The big Mexican raised his black, oily face until Claude had a good sighting at the man's fierce black moustache, and aimed again, confident he'd missed. The Mexican then turned very ponderously toward the three startled *peones* as though to speak to them, and fell. Claude hadn't missed after all.

The *peones* whirled up off the ground, twisting left and right, trying to catch some sign of their leader's assassin. Claude drew his carbine back so there'd be no flash of hot light off cold steel, and put his head too low for it to be made out from down below. The *vaqueros* were confused and excited. They gesticulated and ran around a little, unable to ascertain where that killing bullet had come from. One of them started over toward Clayton. Claude eased his carbine out again, cocked it, and was seeking that one through his sights when one of the others called loudly, gesturing toward the horses. The one farthest off looked from Clayton to his dead *jefe*, then, seeing he was going to be abandoned, turned and ran for his mount. The three of them broke away in a wild rush straight down the middle of the barren cañon, southward.

Claude sat up, fished out a replacement for the one bullet he'd expended, and plugged it into his carbine while watching those fleeing Mexican *peones* growing smaller and smaller. After that he arose, knocked dust and grit off his clothing, and returned to his horse.

He kept the entire cañon in view as he began

angling down off the overhead desert toward the place where Clayton and the dead Mexican lay, within a hundred feet of that shriveled, mummified carcass of a dead horse. Clayton's chestnut saw him and raised its head to nicker softly. The Mexican *jefe*'s animal, also ground-tied nearby, made a soft call to Claude's animal.

He rode slowly and carefully, approaching as he came on in a wide circle the way wary Apaches did when coming on to an enemy they thought was dead but wished to take no chances with. By the time he got up close enough to see where his slug had hit, he marveled that the big Mexican had turned at all. The bullet had pierced him from front to back, right through the center of his chest.

He untied Clayton and hung the dazed man's hat over his face to shield his eyes from the sun, then squatted beside Clayton, patiently awaiting the return to consciousness, and smoked.

The Mexicans were nothing more than a very faint dust banner far southward. The dead one yielded nothing from his pockets but the usual personal effects—a little silver, some tobacco, a bandanna handkerchief. He was a villainous-looking man, pockmarked, scarred, his coarse mouth beneath the big mustache twisted downward even in death. Claude picked up the big knife. It was razor-sharp and nearly a foot long. It had evidently been hammered into shape out of a shoeing rasp because there could still be discerned the very faint criss-crossing lines.

Clayton groaned and moved, rolled his eyes, and knocked aside the shielding hat to find himself gazing at leathery, tough old Claude Rainey, who sat smoking and toying with the big knife. Clayton raised up, winced from the effort, and saw, for the first time, his dead assailant. He spat, raised a hand to feel the side of his face where a purple, sullen lump lay, and said: "What took you so long?"

"Had to shave and have breakfast first," replied Claude laconically. "Besides, how come someone like you needs help, when there were only four of 'em."

Clayton straightened up into a sitting posture, flexed his arms, and gazed around. "At least they didn't get my horse," he croaked.

Claude flipped the knife. It stuck into the ground point first between Clayton's legs. "He wouldn't have done you a particle of good in another hour, mister. Tell me, where were they?"

"They found my horse down in the *jacal*, when I went in to lead him out to water, and jumped on me like a herd of wildcats. All I remember after that was someone holding me in the saddle until I came around on my way over here."

Claude nodded. "One question, Mister Clayton . . . why in the devil does everyone have to come back to this spot? Your partner's dead and buried in town. All that's left out here is that mummified skeleton of his horse."

Clayton looked around again, felt his cheek where the big Mexican had struck him, and afterward massaged his wrists as he said: "Sheriff, this is a guessing game we're all playing. Brìon's assassins must have told him my partner tried to bury the ten thousand dollars here, and from that I'm guessing he thinks the cache of gold bars is around here, too. When I came around after they had me, and saw where we were heading, I figured Brìon himself would be waiting out here. But he wasn't. That big Mexican had evidently been ordered to fetch me here because Brìon figures the cache is somewhere around, and start torturing me to find out exactly where the cache is."

Claude turned this over and over in his mind, then put a shrewd gaze upon the younger, burlier man as he said in a very soft way: "Mister Clayton, just how near to being right were they?"

Clayton stood up gingerly and flexed his legs without answering. He had two bruises, one on the side of his face, one higher up on the opposite side near the hairline. He'd also evidently put up quite a scrap the night before when he'd been jumped in the dark *jacal*, because his shirt was torn and his knuckles were skinned.

Sheriff Rainey stood up, toed the dead Mexican with his foot, and privately debated whether to hoist the hefty devil up behind his saddle and haul him back to town like that, or to come back with a wagon from the livery barn and take him to Boot Hill this other way. He decided to take him back now. He went after his horse, forgetting entirely that the dead man's animal was still around until he looked up and saw the beast. Then he said gruffly: "Give me a hand with Pancho here. He gets his last ride belly-down across his own saddle."

The Mexican was a larger man than he seemed; it took all the strength they both had to get him flung across his saddle. As they were lashing him securely, Arch Clayton looked over at Claude several times without Rainey being aware of it, and as the lawman stepped back to examine critically their tying job Clayton said: "It's close by." He turned to go after his chestnut horse.

Claude gazed after him, wondering, but he didn't ask the obvious question. When they were mounted, Claude leading the dead Mexican's horse, he said: "Mister Clayton, unless I've sized up Fernando Bríon all wrong, the minute those cowboys of his get back down to the *rancho* and tell him what happened up here this morning, he's going to come the next time in person, and if you thought you had trouble before, he's going to make you figure everything previous was a pleasant little game of musical chairs."

Arch Clayton borrowed Claude's makings, twisted up a cigarette, and looked across the dead world to where the sun was high and brassy. "Mighty good sight," he murmured, passing back the tobacco sack. "I didn't figure I'd see it come up this morning. That sun I mean."

They said very little after that, all the way back to town. Claude didn't want to cause a furor so he left the dead Mexican in one of the abandoned *jacales* where Clayton had also been hiding out, took the dead man's horse and outfit to the livery barn along with his own animal, and scowled when the liveryman asked a couple of leading questions. Afterward, Claude and Arch Clayton went up to Barney's store where Arch bought a new shirt, put it on in the back room, then again, avoiding questions by scowling, Claude led off toward the café. It was late for breakfast and early for dinner, but that never kept a man's stomach from growling.

Chapter Seven

Claude Rainey was correct, not that he wanted to be right in this instance, and not that he was certain that he was right. It wasn't until the same stage company clerk, who brought him several letters the following day after he'd saved Clayton over in Dead Man's Cañon, insisted that what the driver had reported wasn't just a bunch of cowboys out looking for cattle.

"Mexicans, Sheriff. I tell you it was at least ten of 'em led by a tall one riding a fancy saddle. Let me tell you . . . when Johnny Egger says he seen a big band of armed Mexicans coming up across the border down below that broad cañon where you found that dead feller, that's exactly what it was. Johnny's one of our best men. He don't make up no tales."

After the clerk had departed, Claude opened his letters. The first one was in response to his earlier letter to the U.S. marshal's office at Phoenix. It confirmed there definitely was a substation up at Raton, New Mexico. It also confirmed there was a part-time—formerly a full-time—deputy marshal up there named Archer Clayton. This letter then went on to recite some of Clayton's triumphs as a lawman.

The second letter was from the Raton, New

71

Mexico, civil authorities. It also confirmed the existence of a field office for the U.S. marshal down at Phoenix. It said about the same thing concerning Arch Clayton, too, except that Raton's civil authorities obviously didn't know nearly as much about Clayton as the U.S. marshal's office over at Phoenix knew, which didn't surprise Claude any.

He put those two letters carefully in a drawer and put the earlier doubts he'd had of Archer Clayton out of his mind. Something a lot more critical had just jumped up to confront him.

He went up to Mather's saloon looking for Clayton, and failed to find him. He then drifted down to the exact opposite end of town and went prowling through the *jacales*. At one time there'd been a strong move on foot to demolish those ancient mud hovels. They had at one time been functional enough, but even when people had been living in them they'd had the ugly appearance of upright mud blocks, and now, many years after the last Mexican had moved out, they clustered down there as immutable, as square and forlorn and ominous-seeming as any set of abandoned mud buildings. No one could even come close to guessing their age. Perhaps a hundred years old, perhaps two hundred, there were no Mexicans around Springville any more. They'd moved on, finding homes in other, all-Mexican communities. In a land where often enough two and three years passed without a drop of rain to wash the mud walls, and in an atmosphere both hot and very dry, wooden buildings were the only structures that time worked upon with dryrot. Mud *jacales* stood forever. In fact, as Claude Rainey walked among them, he began to have an uncanny feeling that maybe the Indians and half-castes used by the conquering Spaniards as their beasts of burden might have lived here.

Then a thick shadow moved and Claude whirled, going for his gun.

"Easy," complained Arch Clayton. "Sheriff, you got to do something about those nerves of yours."

Claude straightened up stiffly. "Very funny," he growled. "I'll tell you something else to split your sides over. Brion and his *vaqueros* are coming. A stage driver saw them cross up out of Mexico about dawn this morning."

"How many?"

Claude shrugged. "He wasn't sure. Ten or twelve maybe. I'd guess, since the stage road lies a good mile and a half from where they crossed over, all he saw was a bunch of Mex *vaqueros*. There could be twenty of them for all he'd know."

"Brion, Sheriff? You're sure it's Brion?"

"No. Of course I'm not sure. That's why I've been looking for you. Let's get mounted and go look for ourselves."

They left Springville, heading northward. Where Claude veered off, southerly now, he said dryly that if they kept up high and Bríon came up into Arizona by way of Dead Man's Cañon, he'd be below them and they'd be able to spot him first.

That's exactly how it worked out, but beyond that Claude found himself incorrect in that earlier syllepsis he'd made; Johnny Egger'd proved his eyesight very well. There weren't any twenty of them as Claude had dourly speculated. There were only ten.

Johnny Egger was right again, too. They had a fancily dressed, very tall, fair-complexioned man on a silver-mounted saddle leading them.

Claude dismounted, took his carbine, and crawled up to the edge of the overhead slope exactly as he'd done when he'd saved Arch Clayton's bacon. There, he growled for Arch to keep low, and he pointed southward where the riders were coming upcountry at a leisurely walk.

"Ten," murmured Clayton, "and sure as hell that's Fernando Bríon out front." He looked at Claude. "Those three *peones* sure didn't let any grass grow under them. They had to ride hard all yesterday and part of last night to reach Bríon's *hacienda*."

Claude had an observation along those lines, too. He said: "*Amigo*, it's not how hard those cowboys rode getting home that's interesting me right now. It's how hard Bríon rode back, to

74

get into Dead Man's Cañon." Rainey cocked a jaundiced eye at Clayton. "You sure you didn't tell them anything when that big one was knocking you down and threatening you with his knife?"

Clayton didn't even bother answering that. He simply threw a withering look at Sheriff Rainey, then resumed his vigil.

The Mexicans were armed with carbines, six-guns, knives, and their crossed bandoleers. They looked less like cowboys and more like a little party of guerillas, which, as a matter of fact, they also were. In times of peace, guerillas worked as *vaqueros* on Mexico's immense cattle ranches. In times of war or insurrection, without changing even their hats, they became irregular cavalry.

Fernando Bríon alone among those men coming up into the broad expanse of Dead Man's Cañon wore the short, elaborately embroidered riding jacket of the Mexican *charro*—gentleman horseman. He also wore the gold-thread-encrusted large, peaked sombrero. His saddle with its dinner-plate horn and white goat-rawhide covered tree had silver inlay upon the heavy steel stirrups, upon the horn cap, even upon the ornate cantle and swells. Also, the stock of the Winchester carbine jutting up under Bríon's right leg was carved and silver inlaid. Yellow sunlight flashed from Bríon's clothing and equipment, prompting Sheriff Rainey to wag his head and grumble under his breath that any man who got decked out like that deserved to be shot; watchers could see him for two miles before they even got close enough to ambush him.

Clayton's reaction was different. He'd evidently taken only cursory inventory of Brion's dress and accoutrements. It was the tall, handsome, fair-skinned man himself Clayton was intently watching.

"Give me another fifteen minutes, until he gets into range, Sheriff, and I'll make him look like a bundle of red-flecked rags with my Winchester."

Claude pushed steadily backward until he was far enough from the slope to stand up without being seen from down below. "You'll do no such a damned thing," he said. "We've got to have something more than another damned corpse to tie him to three corpses . . . your partner, Jonas Gantt, and that Mexican raider you buried." Claude jerked his head and started back where the horses waited. "I know how you feel. I'm not even saying that if Brion and I were the only ones within a hundred miles on a good day for sighting that I wouldn't be tempted to kill him. But we're not going to do it. At least not just yet. Now let's get back to town."

They left, galloping swiftly along the overhead desert until it was safe to slacken off and walk their mounts through the reddening afternoon.

"He'll show himself," said Claude. "He's got to

show himself, otherwise he's not going to learn anything. He's also got to find you, Clayton."

"That's not going to be easy the second time."

"No," agreed Sheriff Rainey, "it sure isn't. Because I'm charging you with attempted murder so I can lock you up in my jailhouse. Believe me, that's the only building in Springville those sly rascals of his can't break into, blast you out of, or shoot through the windows and skewer you to the wall."

Clayton looked surprised initially, then afterward, as he slouched along thinking this over, he looked less surprised and more skeptical.

Claude said something else, obviously spoken to turn aside some of Arch Clayton's uneasiness. "We've had a vigilance committee in Springville for the past five years. We formed it when Mex raiders used to come a-helling up over the line trying to stampede horses and cattle down on to the Tamaulipas Plains. After we caught a couple of those little bands, shot a few, hanged a few, and got the others a nice long stretch in the Tucson penitentiary, they quit coming. Since then we've sort of let things slide. But the minute I get back to town I'll pass the word. Then, let Mister Bryan . . . or Bree-own . . . come riding on in. We simply close off both ends of the roadway, guard the side roads, and there he sits like a duck on a pond . . . he can have it any old way he wants it, but the first corpse will be his."

Evening was settling by the time they reached town. They split up, Clayton to take his horse and equipment over to the livery barn from the *jacal* where he'd been keeping them, and Claude Rainey up to Mather's saloon to mention quietly to Jack bad trouble might be impending from a band of Mexican gunmen who were approaching from the southwest, suggesting that Mather, former chieftain of the vigilantes, might send out word for the men to meet at his place as soon as they could get there.

After that, Claude met Arch Clayton, and they went together to the café for supper. It was by then not quite 8:00, with plenty of daylight left over although the sun had been gone for nearly two hours.

Claude was gloomy or introspective or perhaps both because he was quiet all through the meal, even when Clayton made a couple of mild comments. But afterward, when they were outside in the hot night looking up and down the roadway where lights showed and people moved with more alacrity than they'd shown during the blast furnace days, Claude pointed toward his office and said: "I reckon Mister Brion'll be looking for us down there, when he gets his crew safely tucked away, so we might as well go down, get comfortable, and wait."

The jailhouse was cooler even than the night, which was the primary advantage of three-foot thick mud walls. Claude had one fairly large strap-steel cage set across his back wall. There was no partition, and from the looks of the dust inside there hadn't been a prisoner locked up for some time. Clayton assessed that cage. "Big enough for ten men, I'd say," he murmured.

Claude looked up, his gaze wry. "A man has to be standing up to lock 'em into it," he said. "The fellow who owns the saloon up the road offered me a bet a few days back that you'd be killed like Gantt was, down in Mexico. Well, I'd update that a mite, if I was a betting man, and say tonight's the night." Claude nodded grimly toward the door. "You poke your nose out there an hour from now and they'll be watching like barn owls. Only this time they won't waste a lot of time slapping you around, Clayton. If Brión's up here to do the job himself, I'll bet you a month's pay he could wring it out of you in less than thirty minutes."

Clayton didn't dispute this. All he said was: "Locking me up isn't going to solve anything, not with that damned cell out in plain sight. If Brión knows where I am, that'll be two-thirds of the battle for him."

Claude nodded, got out of his chair, and went over to move a heavy bench. "Come here," he said, then bent, caught a mighty iron ring set into the floor, and heaved. "Give me a hand," he gasped. "This damned thing hasn't been raised in more years than I like to think back on."

"What is it?" asked Clayton, leaning to catch hold and also strain upward, lifting a section of the floor out.

Claude eased the door against the wall and panted. "Hole in the ground," he said, dryly. "If you figure those old Mex *jacales* at the south end of town are all that remains of the Spanish and Mexican days, this'll prove you're wrong." He pointed. It was dark as the inside of a well down below. The air rising from down there was musty and stale. "Climb down, Mister Clayton. No one, including Fernando Brion, will see you down there."

Arch bent, then dropped to one knee, struck a match, and peered at the hole beneath him. It seemed to be about ten or twelve feet square. The walls were smooth earth dubbed with rock. There was an old ladder leading down. Arch reared back and looked up.

Claude said: "The ladder'll hold you. Just climb down, and don't make any noise or smoke. If Brion comes calling, I won't know very much about you, least of all where you are now."

Clayton swung over a leg, gingerly eased his weight down upon the ancient rungs of the rawhide-wrapped ladder, and said: "Sheriff, have you looked down into this damned dungeon with a lamp lately?"

"No, why?"

"Why? Well, I'll tell you why, confound it,

because tarantulas and Gila monsters and even rattlesnakes look for places just like this when it gets too hot outside for them. That's why."

Claude stroked his bristly chin and never so much as twinkled his eyes as he replied: "Come to think on it, you're dead right, Mister Clayton. Now ease the other leg down. That's fine. I'll set the bench back over the door and no one'll have any idea you're down here." Clayton was half-way down. Claude bent to watch. "By the way," he said. "It takes two to lift the trap door, so if anything happens to me, you might be in a little trouble. You see, no one can hear you yelling from down in there."

Claude had one last glimpse of Clayton's startled expression, dropped the massive door back into place, shoved the bench over it, and there was no evidence at all that Archer Clayton had ever been in the room.

Rainey then resumed his position at the desk, tossed aside his hat, raised his feet, and tipped back the chair, all ready to wait, no matter how long it took, for Fernando Brion to come calling.

Chapter Eight

Barney Whitsun showed up a half hour later, looked around, stepped in, and sank into a chair, looking troubled. "What's it all about?" he asked. "Jack sent me word, and when I got up to the saloon, hell, nearly all the other fellers was either up there already or, like Mister Douglas, had been sent word outside of town and probably are on their way in. What we'd like to know is what's happening, Claude?"

Rainey had a flip answer. "So would I, Barney. All I can tell you right now is that a band of Mexican gunmen crossed the border this morning, heading for Springville, and to make sure Johnny Egger was right, I rode out myself and scouted 'em up."

"They're real, Claude?"

"They're plumb real, Barney. Ten of 'em led by a tall Mex named Fernando Brion."

"Brion, Brion. Say, isn't that the name of the one who fetched Gantt's stuff back here out of Mexico?"

"Yeah. Same man. Barney, I think he just might be after that ten thousand dollars."

Claude didn't think that at all but he wanted to get rid of Whitsun before Brion walked in, and

82

since Barney had to tell the vigilantes up at Jack's bar something, he told the general store owner that lie. But it wasn't just a spur-of-the-moment prevarication. Since Claude had first mentioned a fine little schoolhouse for Springville, the idea had caught on with alacrity. Of course, the only way Springville would ever get such a building would be if that $10,000 could be legally acquired. When Barney returned to the saloon and related what he'd been told down at the jailhouse, the town's temper would rise quickly. Springville had only the sketchiest claim to that money, but some fancy clan of a Mexican had no claim at all, so Jack Mather's vigilantes would sit up there, talking and drinking and slowly coming to a boiling wrath.

After Barney departed, Claude stood in the doorway of his office wondering whether he had time to go fetch himself a mug of coffee. He decided he did have, went to the café, got a bottle of java, a cup to drink it with, and returned to the jailhouse.

Again, as always, it was the confounded waiting. He sipped coffee and smoked, leaving his road-way door partially open, cocked up his feet upon the desk and reviewed the interesting things that had occurred recently. He was still like that, hat on the back of his head, leathery, sun-tanned countenance creased in thought, when a hand reached forth out of the night to ease the roadway door open farther, and Fernando Bríon stepped inside.

Claude Rainey was no actor. Like most men deeply honest, pretense, like any other variety of deceit, just did not come easily to him, and since he didn't like it in himself, he didn't like it in others. He nodded at Bríon, showing neither surprise at his presence in Springville, nor pleasure at his presence in the jailhouse.

Bríon's dark, very intelligent eyes raked over Claude's features, and as the handsome Mexican stepped to a chair and sat down in it, removing his hat as he did so, it wouldn't have been at all difficult for the Mexican to sense in the hostile atmosphere that Sheriff Claude Rainey knew more than Bríon had previously suspected that he might.

"You're not surprised to see me," he said pleasantly, and eased back in the chair. "That means, then, that you were told I was coming. Congratulations, Sheriff, on the sound eyesight of your *compadres* around this town."

Claude sipped coffee, eyed the younger man, and said nothing. Bríon had closed the roadside door. They were alone. Well, they were *almost* alone. Beneath their chairs was another man, but he couldn't hear anything they were saying, or even know that Bríon was above him, for that matter, or so Claude thought.

Bríon swept his intent, dark glance over

84

Rainey's features a time or two, evidently trying to guess where he should begin, how much Rainey already knew, and how much he only thought he knew. Finally, in order to begin somewhere, he put out a gentle feeler.

"I was visited a few days back by a *yanqui* from northern New Mexico. A man named Archer Clayton. So you know him, Sheriff?"

"I know him," stated Claude, putting aside his half-full coffee cup. "He was around town yesterday for a while."

"I see. He was also around town today, no?"

"I've been almighty busy the last few days, Mister Brîon. It'd take a whole herd of sheriffs to keep watch on everyone hereabouts."

Brîon smiled. "Of course, *amigo*. But you didn't answer my question, so I'll ask another one. Do you know why he is down in your part of the country?"

Claude was wearying of this. Moreover, he suspected the Mexican was more than his match at fencing with words, so he said bluntly: "Something to do with some old Spanish gold coins you bought from him and his partner. His partner's the dead man I buried a while back. That's his dead horse out there in the cañon."

Brîon's eyes brightened. He was finding out, he thought, what Rainey knew, and up to a point at least, that simplified things for him. "*Sí,* you are correct, Sheriff Rainey."

"Brion," exclaimed Claude, reaching up to square the hat atop his head, "when you came here before, bringing Jonas Gantt's guns and other stuff, I figured you were something better by a damned sight than you're turning out to be! You didn't have to send those *vaqueros* of yours out to shoot that U.S. deputy marshal. If you'd just disarmed him and sent him back over the line, you'd have achieved your end just as well."

Brion wasn't the least bit ruffled by Rainey's bluntness or his show of anger, but he no longer smiled when he replied. "Sheriff, I've seen them before, those deputy U.S. lawmen. They don't give up. In my country we know from long experience that two kinds of *gringos* have to be shot to be diverted. Texans, and U.S. marshals. Also, in my country, it's perfectly legal to shoot them, so if you're thinking of arresting me . . . don't try it. I've committed no crime in the United States. You couldn't hold me an hour."

Claude stamped out his cigarette. "You don't know as much U.S. law as you seem to figure you do," he stated. "I wouldn't have to lock you up for Gantt's killing, Mister Brion. I'd only have to lock you up for the murder of that young fellow you gave the ten thousand dollars to, because he was killed in Arizona, not Mexico."

Brion gently shook his head, showing that very gentle smile again. "But I didn't kill that one, Sheriff. You'd never in this world be able to prove it. I could produce fifty . . . a hundred and fifty . . . witnesses that I was at the town of Rosario near my ranch, when that one was killed." Bríon paused, eyed Claude Rainey as a cat eyes a cornered mouse, then he said: "Forget these things, Sheriff. All they do is cloud the issue between us. I've heard from travelers down around Rosario, that you want that ten thousand dollars you've impounded, and which is locked up in that ridiculous iron box over at the general store here in Springville." Bríon leaned a little as though what he proposed to say next was vitally important to him, which it was. "Sheriff, I'm here to make you a present of that ten thousand dollars." Bríon sat there, waiting for Rainey's reaction to this. He particularly watched Claude's eyes for a shadow of cupidity to appear. When it didn't, he said: "In exchange for my assignment of all that money to you, I want you to hand Archer Clayton over to me." Bríon eased back in his chair again, watching Claude closely.

There was no longer much point, in Claude's opinion, for holding this conversation with gloves on. They both understood one another perfectly. Claude considered the handsome, younger man with a cold stare before he said: "Bríon, you're kidding yourself. I know about the map and the marks on the gold coins."

Bríon's eyes suddenly popped wide open. "Map?" he murmured. "What map?"

Claude saw at once he'd been careless. Obviously Brión knew about the marks on the coins, but he either didn't believe anyone else knew of them, or their purpose, or he hadn't yet assumed that, since someone else knew what those marks meant, someone had drawn a map from them. Claude bit his lip, but it was too late to retract, so he plunged straight ahead and told the truth.

"The map to that cache of old-time Spanish gold, Brión. The same cache that's resulted in four deaths so far, and will probably result in a hell of a lot more deaths before anyone finds that lousy gold."

Brión was troubled now. "Four . . . ? Sheriff, Gantt and the man trying to get away with the ten thousand dollars, but what other men have died?"

"A big Mexican you sent to lead those assassins up here to torture the truth out of Clayton. He's dead. If your *peones* didn't tell you about him, then I'm surprised at them."

"Oh," said Brión, with an indifferent, cold flick of the fingers. "Him. Well, of course. I'd forgotten. And the fourth man, Sheriff Rainey?"

"A bushwhacker Arch Clayton brought back here with him. Another of your men. He died from a gunshot wound through the lungs."

Brión's expression changed. He seemed almost relieved, but only briefly, as though he'd wondered as to where this man had disappeared.

Then, with a dark suspicion crossing his mind, dark enough also to make a shadow pass across his face, Brion said: "He told you . . . what?"

"All he knew, Brion. That you had Jonas Gantt assassinated. That you also had the fellow with the ten thousand dollars followed and killed up here in Arizona. He also said he worked for you."

Brion nodded; all the little questions in his mind were being answered one by one. It became very clear now, that Brion understood the extent of Claude Rainey's knowledge. He flicked a cold and steady stare over at the lawman. "Sheriff," he said very softly, "you're a man who doesn't give much of an impression for intelligence. I can see where that's definitely in your favor."

"You better also see something else, *amigo*," Claude growled. "You're not going out of this jailhouse."

Brion wasn't disturbed by that. He brushed it aside to ask another question. "Forget me for now, Sheriff, and tell me frankly whether my offer of the ten thousand dollars appeals to you? A man your age can travel a very long way on ten thousand dollars. He can lose himself in this huge land, buy a house somewhere, and spend the best years of his life living well and comfortably."

Claude snorted in derision. "In the first place, Brion, that ten thousand dollars doesn't even belong to you. In the second place, I wouldn't accept the bribe even if it did. And in the third place, you're no longer in a position to offer any kind of a trade. Maybe you were down at Rosario when that fellow got the top of his head shot off down in Dead Man's Cañon, but in Arizona we got a law dealing with what we call 'an accessory after the fact', which means, since you sent those bushwhackers up here to kill that fellow and steal back the ten thousand you paid him for those damned gold coins, that we can hold you and try you as though you actually pulled the trigger yourself."

Brion raised a hand and carelessly tapped the back wall where he was sitting, beside the roadway door. He then said: "Sheriff, I know about that law of yours."

The door opened and three dark and murderous-looking Mexicans stepped through on quiet feet, pushing cocked pistols toward Sheriff Rainey. They would shoot in a second; their eyes and their slitted mouths said as much. Brion stood up, lazily, and reached for his hat. He made no move toward the six-gun he wore. He didn't have to, under the circumstances.

He said: "Sorry, Sheriff, but I can't stay. I'm on the trail of Arch Clayton. I'll find him, because even if he left your town as you seem to want me to believe, I've already sent half my men upcountry in the direction of Raton to intercept him." Brion flashed his handsome smile, put on his big sombrero, brushed the brim with his fingers, and stepped back out through the doorway into the darkened night beyond. "¡*Adiós, muchacho!*" he called, and disappeared.

For fully five minutes the armed Mexicans stood inside, covering Claude Rainey, then they, too, left.

Claude looked at his cold coffee, drank it, swore heartily, and didn't even bother going outside to look up and down the roadway. They were gone; Bríon wasn't the kind who left loose ends lying around.

Claude went over, moved the bench, stamped loudly as a signal for Arch Clayton to push upward from below, then he bent, grasped the ring, and heaved backward. The floor groaned and moved, then suddenly, as though someone below had just heaved a thick shoulder, it flew open and Clayton climbed out. Without a word passing between them, they eased the door down, put the bench back into place, and straightened up, regarding each other.

Claude said: "Could you hear anything from down there?"

Clayton's reply was crisp. "There's a chiseled out slit someone made right beneath where your desk sits, Sheriff. By standing straight, a man can put his ear up to it. Yeah, I heard."

"Well . . . he out-foxed me."

Clayton was laconic about that. "One thing I've

learned about Mexicans, Sheriff . . . when they're smiling and all relaxed . . . look out."

Claude went back and peered into his coffee container. It still held a little of the cold brew. He stonily refilled the cup and held it out. Clayton took it, went to the very chair Bríon had used, sat down, and sipped. He was silent for a long time. So was Claude Rainey, but with Claude it was chagrin more than speculation that kept him that way. At fifty-five a man with his experience should have suspected that fancy-Dan wouldn't just walk in and expect just to walk out again. Now he had a *personal* score to settle with Fernando Bríon. Before, he'd had only professional interest in the man.

"All right," he eventually growled. "I'll get the vigilantes and we'll go Mexican hunting."

"Wait a minute!" exclaimed Clayton, setting aside the emptied cup. "Let's just sit and figure for a spell, Sheriff. Anyway, you'd never find them. Bríon's anything but a fool. Sit back, relax. Let's do some quiet figuring."

Chapter Nine

The entire drama fell into place when the two men fitted each scene into perspective. Only two things were fresh to their minds and worth careful study and re-study, because one of them at least changed everything.

As far as Brion's remark about sending half his men northeastward toward Raton, that didn't mean much unless Brion should recall them, then, according to Claude Rainey, Brion would have a pretty big force of cut-throats at his back. In any event, Claude knew exactly how to deal with a situation like that. He'd been pitting force against force most of his life.

But what really honed their dilemma to a razor's edge of danger was the careless remark Claude had made about someone having already figured out, by drawing a map and integrating those marks off the coins, where that old-time Spanish cache was.

Brion didn't have enough of the coins to do that yet himself, and he'd never get enough coins now to do it, so it didn't take much of a discussion for Claude and Arch Clayton to guess what Brion had to do now—catch Clayton.

"That simple," growled Claude. "I ought to be kicked for letting that slip out the way I did. But he irritated me, sitting there, looking rich and calm and untroubled about the men he'd caused to die."

"It's that simple all right," agreed Clayton. "He wants me right this minute more than he wants even that damned cache." Clayton peered into the cup, into the coffee container, found them both empty, and stood up to say he was hungry.

Claude jumped up with a low growl. "You just bar the door behind me. I'll go fetch us both some grub. You're not going out of here. Boy, don't sell Brion short. He'll have eyes out there in the night all around this building just like he'll have other eyes hunting through the dark corners of town."

Arch barred the door behind Sheriff Rainey and resumed his seat. Fifteen minutes later, when Claude returned, he hadn't moved. "I've got an idea," he said, as he let Claude back inside and leaned his back upon the door. "We'll round up your vigilantes from the saloon yonder, take some lanterns, my map, and go dig up that damned cache, fetch it back here to town, and keep it where Brion wouldn't stand a chance of getting it."

Claude didn't say anything right away. He divided up their food and coffee, sat down at his desk, and dropped his old hat atop a pile of papers as he began to eat.

Clayton didn't touch his food. He waited for

Sheriff Rainey to comment. He fished inside a shirt pocket, brought forth a small, badly worn little black notebook, and tossed it over by Claude's hat atop the desk. Rainey's eyes took in the little book slowly.

"The map in there?" he asked, around a mouthful of food.

Clayton nodded, still waiting.

Claude put down his sandwich and reached with his right hand for the cup of coffee. He never made it. Neither did he answer Clayton, for the door that Arch hadn't barred from the inside after Sheriff Rainey's return slowly opened, and silently the same three murderous-eyed Mexicans who had come in out of the night once before stepped in soundlessly out of the night, shuffled back into shadows away from the door, their cocked six-guns covering Clayton and Rainey.

Fernando Brion stepped through moments later. There wasn't a movement or a sound in the jailhouse as Clayton and Rainey raised their eyes, sitting like stone. Brion gently closed the door and leaned upon it, looking with his darkly triumphant stare at Archer Clayton. He smiled.

"No man as lean as Sheriff Rainey would eat all the food and drink from two cups all the coffee he brought back from the little café, *amigos*."

Brion swept an indifferent glance over where his black-eyed killers stood poised for an order to start shooting. He let his glance slip on past and probe the room, then he shrugged as though to himself; as though he still didn't understand how Claude had hidden Arch Clayton, but as though it wasn't really important now anyway. Then he stepped away from the door, crossed to the wall bench and sat down, pushed his long legs out, and stonily regarded Clayton.

"A man with as much to lose as I have," he told Arch, "takes no chances. Of course, I had my men hiding and watching. You were foolish ever to think otherwise, *Señor* Clayton."

"I didn't think otherwise," contradicted Arch, his right hand a good two feet away from his right hip where the lashed-down six-gun jutted from its holster.

"No? Well then," murmured Bríon, switching his attention to Claude Rainey. "You were foolish to bring all that food back here within sight of my spies, Sheriff, for it doesn't take a very smart man to figure out two portions of everything mean two men are to eat, and since my spies reported no one had entered the jailhouse after I left it, why then naturally I knew you'd had Clayton hidden in here all the time." Bríon made a little gesture of contempt. "The *yanqui* mind, *amigos*, is full of fight, yes, but it has never been very clever in other ways."

Claude finally recovered, and looked at Arch with troubled eyes. "That's the second time I pulled a damned fool stunt," he growled.

Brion said: "*Señor* Clayton, you made a map, Sheriff Rainey told me. Fine, otherwise I was going to have to take you up to Raton for the rest of the coins, then kill you and work up my own map. This way I'm saved a lot of time and hard riding. Tell me, where is this map?"

Clayton's eyes didn't so much as flicker. Claude, sitting with his outstretched arm lightly lying upon the desk not six inches from the little black book, picked up his hat, put it on his head, and waited like that for Clayton's answer. Brion was also waiting, his face expressionless, his liquid dark eyes like black stones.

"Near Raton," lied Arch. "So you didn't get saved the hard ride after all."

For several terrible seconds the silence settled and grew out thin again. Brion slapped his leg and leaned as though to arise. "Then we have to take the sheriff with us," he said, arising, looking balefully down at his prisoners. "Other-wise he'll send an alarm to Raton, and maybe even round up some of those fools sitting around over at the saloon waiting for . . . they know not what . . . but he knows, and I know, and you know."

Claude removed his hat, tossed it down angrily on top of the little black notebook, and started to jump up. One of the villainous Mexicans snarled and tipped up his pistol. Claude glared, but eased back down again, gripping both arms of his desk chair.

97

"You've got things figured out just fine," he snapped at Bríon. "But those men you spied out up there at the saloon'll be on your trail before sunup when they find me missing . . . or dead."

Bríon seemed momentarily to consider this, then he jerked his head at the nearest Mexican assassin and said in swift Spanish: "Little one, this old man I believe we must kill. But not with the pistol for the noise will be formidable. Do you possess a knife?"

In the same language the Mexican said that he had, indeed, an excellent knife; it was soundless and very sharp.

Clayton and Rainey, understanding this soft exchange, tensed for action and Bríon noticed that, so he faced them anew, speaking once more in English. "Don't try it, *amigos*. I didn't say we *wouldn't* shoot you. All I said was that it would make a lot of noise."

"You're bucking a losing streak," growled Claude. "You kill me and you'll never get safely back to Mexico."

Bríon acknowledged the disposal of Claude Rainey was a problem, but he didn't act too concerned about it. He even showed that gentle little smile again as he said: "Sheriff, one thing I've always admired is a brave man. So we'll take you with us on your own horse so no one around Springville will notice anything odd until we're too far away to be caught, then we'll give you the

Mexican *fuego*." Bríon raised his eyebrows. "You know what I'm talking about?"

Claude knew. Every *yanqui* in the Southwest knew. It was an old Mexican tradition, and while it definitely did show respect for a brave man, it nevertheless was quite fatal. A prisoner wasn't turned about and shot in the back the way cravens and outlaws were executed; he was, instead, permitted one almost non-existent chance for his life. The executioners lined up, the captive was told to run, and he was allowed sometimes as much as a two-hundred-foot start, before the gunmen tried to kill him. The number of men who'd lived through that experience in over a hundred years of Mexican application could all be counted upon the fingers of one hand. Still, it was considered homage to bravery to be given the chance.

Sheriff Rainey slowly arose. "Let's go," he snapped.

Bríon gazed at him. So did Clayton. They both seemed to harbor the notion that Claude Rainey wasn't at all resigned, but had instead concocted some evasive notion in his head. Clayton arose, then, and upset all Bríon's speculations with one statement.

"Wait a minute. Bríon, how badly do you want that cache of Spanish gold?"

The handsome Mexican's black gaze shifted and turned gradually sharp as the gaze of a ferret.

He had guessed what Arch would say, but he went along with it anyway.

"You can guess, *amigo*, how badly. I've sent four men to their deaths and will happily kill five times that many more. So speak out, I'm listening."

"I can remember every twist and turn on that map in my head. We won't have to ride to Raton. I can take you where the cache is. It'll take most of the night, but by sunup we should be there."

Bríon nodded very slightly, gazing straight at Arch Clayton. "I see. And in return for showing me the cache, you want Sheriff Rainey spared. Is that correct?"

"Yes."

"*Amigo*," purred the Mexican. "If you know, I can torture it out of you. I don't have to bargain for . . ."

"You're dead wrong, Bríon. Torture and be damned to you. You kill Rainey and you might just as well kill me, too, because so help me Hannah, you can rip out my tongue and I'll bleed to death and still never tell you."

Clayton's square jaw was locked down hard. The look in his eyes was blackly adamant. Anyone, including Claude Rainey, who saw him standing like that, had to believe he meant exactly what he said. Bríon stood thoughtfully glowering at Clayton, his lips pursed, his eyes darkly smoldering. Then he seemed to arrive at a decision. He said: "Tell me, are you sure you can take us to the cache even in the night?"

Clayton's answer sounded truthful even to Sheriff Rainey. "That's the one big problem. I've never had a chance yet to hunt up the cache, or I'd be able to ride right to it, night or day. That's why I said a minute ago we'd reach it about sunup. I *think* I can do it in the dark, but daylight would sure be a whole lot better."

Bríon turned thoughtful again, still balefully watching. "All right," he assented softly. "But we take Sheriff Rainey with us."

Clayton's jaw closed down like iron again. "No we don't. You can tie him and hide him so he can't get loose for a day or two, but you don't take him with us to shoot later on."

Bríon rammed his fisted hands deeply into his trouser pockets. He had a dilemma and he knew it. He looked at his cowboys, but they didn't understand any of this because it was all being said in English. He gazed at Claude Rainey, then straight at Arch Clayton again. Finally he nodded his head ever so slightly.

"On your terms," he growled, and turned with a harsh order toward his gunmen.

At once two of them put up their pistols and started for Claude Rainey. As they approached him, Bríon said: "Sheriff, if you think your friend has saved your life, don't crow too loudly just yet. If he doesn't take me to the cache, I can still return even in broad daylight, and slit your scrawny gullet." He gestured to the Mexicans. "Tie him," he snarled in Spanish. "And tie him well, little ones, for if he isn't tied and we have to come back this way, of a specific certainty I'll eat the hearts of both of you."

The Mexicans were rough at their work, but they were also obviously skilled. They used Claude's trouser belt, his shell belt, and even his neckerchief and handkerchief to bind him. Clayton watched, as did Bríon, the latter smiling at Sheriff Rainey's grimaces of pain as his tormentors bore down at their work. When they were finished, they only lacked one thing—a gag for Claude's mouth. Bríon handed them a handkerchief from his own pocket, immaculate and of tough linen. "Let him try chewing through that," he said in English to Arch Clayton.

One of the kneeling men asked a question. Bríon didn't answer right away; he turned, gazed into the big strap-steel cage, then went on probing the room for the best place to store Sheriff Rainey. Finally he said, in Spanish, since there was no suitable place indoors, they should haul Rainey around back where an abandoned horse shed stood, and toss him out there. Then, to Clayton, Bríon said: "All right, *amigo*, I've kept my part of the bargain. Now let's see if you will keep your part."

As the Mexicans eased open the door to make

certain it was safe to pass out into the night with their burden, Clayton and Claude Rainey exchanged a long look. Bríon saw and nodded gently.

"Very touching," he said, and reached for Arch's six-gun, straightened back holding the gun, then carelessly tossed it atop the desk beside Sheriff Rainey's hat. "Stand up," he ordered Clayton, and as the grunting Mexicans lugged Claude Rainey outside, Bríon gestured. "Walk out, act perfectly natural, my friend, and follow those men around behind the jailhouse where we left our horses. I'll send one of my men to steal a mount for you, then we'll be on our way."

When the men moved outside that little moon was up there, but it wasn't much thicker than it had been the night before, so the night was as dark as ever.

Chapter Ten

Where Bríon's men dumped Claude there was a jutting stone. It gouged him hard but he made no effort to roll off it until he was certain the Mexicans were gone.

He heard Bríon and Arch Clayton walk by outward bound toward the yonder alleyway. He also heard Bríon instruct one of his men to go steal a saddled horse from one of the tie racks out front. After that, although he knew they were still back there, except for the abrasive rub of leather over leather and the soft music of rein chains and spur rowels, there was no more talk. Finally, however, when the Mexican returned leading a saddled horse, Bríon's last command was given.

"Mount up, Mister Clayton. Eusebio, lead out, and be very careful. Stay in the alleyway until we're out of their town."

Claude heaved himself off the rock and lay panting for a moment. He had very little hope of wrenching loose from the way those experienced *vaqueros* had trussed him up, and back there in his office while he'd been able to do so, he'd fervently hoped they'd put him in the cell, or roll him into a corner, for then Barney or Mather or someone would surely have come along sooner or later to release him. But this place where he now was had been disused for so long the chance of an impromptu discovery was even too remote for him to hope for.

He knew the shed, had in fact used it for his horse up until two years previous. It was rickety and musty and strong-smelling from rats and mice. Although it stood less than a hundred feet behind the jailhouse, in his present view he thought it could've been a hundred miles for all the good distance might do him.

He lay relaxed for a moment thinking what should be done. After he got free, he'd get the vigilantes, of course, and at the first shade of dawn track Bríon down. He groaned; by the first shade of dawn Arch Clayton would be dead.

He heaved around, seeking something he might rely upon to cut through the trouser belt holding his wrists tightly behind his back. There was nothing; even the manger was shiny-smooth from his horse having rubbed on it. There were no protruding nails either; he'd been careful of them and had diligently pounded them back when they'd appeared so his horse wouldn't be snagged. There was nothing at all he might rub against and free himself.

He tried cocking himself upright so he could lean his back upon the manger. It took a lot of straining but he eventually did that, and at least in this somewhat more normal position he could think clearly.

Barney Whitsun and the others, waiting up at Mather's place, would ultimately weary and become impatient. In his own desperation he cursed them for not being more impatient and coming right now, to stamp around in his office.

That was his only hope for salvation, or, more properly, that was the only hope for saving Arch Clayton. He speculated on how to draw the attention of the vigilantes when they eventually came to the jailhouse. Straight in front of him was a propped up post that had rotted off at the ground four or five years earlier.

He'd always intended to replace it but never had; instead, he'd leaned another post against it to keep the rickety little warped wooden shed wall from collapsing outward. The longer he leaned there gazing at that post, because there was nothing else to gaze at, the more he began figuring out an ideal way to attract attention.

There was some peril involved for a man who was inside the little shed and who couldn't move quickly or far when the wall fell because he was tightly bound. He studied the wall, the rotten post, the cant and lean of the partition, and was convinced, if he kicked the supporting post clear, the wall would fall outward. If he guessed wrong and it fell *inward* . . . He shrugged. Since there was no alternative, he'd have to take that chance.

Time ran on, seemingly without end. Claude tried to guess how long it had been since Brion had left town with his captive, and estimated it at roughly two hours. He swore violently behind his linen gag. What in tarnation was keeping those idiots up at Jack's saloon from coming down to seek him?

They came; he heard their loud, angry voices before they even flung open his office door and stamped inside. He even heard one of them swear because the sheriff was missing. He got scooted as low as he could, raised both lashed legs and rested them upon the supporting cedar post, tested the thing and found it solid, tested it a little harder and made the whole warped old wall shiver.

Someone had walked back out of the office accompanied by other men. He heard that garrulous voice say: "Hell no, he ain't far off or he'd have taken his hat. You know as well as I do, Claude Rainey wouldn't be caught dead without his hat."

He slowly straightened his legs from the knee, slowly heaved his weight against the upright post. The wall groaned, boards popped, dust belched downward from the overhang roof. Claude pushed hard, outward, and bit down hard upon his gag with the effort. There was a creaking groan from the overhead rafters. He paused to roll up his eyes. He hadn't counted on the whole roof falling in. He looked to make certain when the wall went he had a clear path to roll back up as close as he could get to the protective side of the cribbed manger. It was going to be dangerous at best.

He sucked back a slow, deep-down big lungful of air and struck out, making his body rigid. The support post broke loose, the wall buckled with a sound as loud as a pistol shot, then it fell outward, which was exactly as Claude had intended for it to do. But the roof, no longer adequately supported, creaked ominously as it began very slowly to fall in. By looking straight upward before slow-rising dust filled the little shed, Claude could see the nails pulling loose up there. They were, for all their age, bright as daggers and pointing directly at him.

He heard someone let off a startled squawk from around front as he frantically rolled like a cocoon up against the manger. But the roof only sagged; it never did let go. At least not while Sheriff Rainey was inside the shed.

Someone with a deep, rough voice ran back to the shed, looked in, and Claude, straining and breathless, saw the astonished face of burly Jack Mather. Jack reared back and yelled to the others.

"Hey, the damned fool's napping in this old shed!"

Claude's neck swelled and he almost strangled on his anger behind the gag as the others came trooping back. Barney Whitsun and big old raw-boned Newton Douglas bent nearly double to peer in at him. Newton exploded a hard curse, grabbed Claude by the shoulders, and bodily tugged him out where they could all crowd up and see him. "Well don't just stand there, god dammit," snarled the cowman. "You can see he's trussed up. Set him free."

They removed the gag last, which was just as well, for by then Claude's blood pressure had dropped considerably. He tried to spring up and had to lean upon Newt Douglas's big arm as circulation began painfully to return to his extremities.

"Get your horses and guns," he gasped at them. "That damned Mexican slipped into town and took Arch Clayton right out of my jailhouse."

Douglas peered down. "What damned Mexican?" he mildly asked.

Claude jerked away. "Fernando Bríon, that's what damned . . . Just go get your horses and guns. I'll explain on the trail. Meet me down at the livery barn where I'll saddle up and be waiting."

They scattered, finally, galvanized into sudden movement by the intensity of Sheriff Rainey's fiery look and angry words. Newt Douglas loped along behind the younger men bellowing for his cowboys to get mounted.

Claude returned to the jailhouse for his booted carbine. He still had that extra carton of Winchester bullets in his pocket he'd taken with him that morning he'd gone down to Dead Man's Cañon to save Clayton's bacon from the big Mexican.

By the time he'd trotted to the livery barn and shouted for the night hawk to saddle and bridle his private mount, the tingling sensation was gone from his limbs. He still ached though, and probably would continue to do so for several days, but he ignored that and kept ranting at the bewildered night hostler to hurry up at the saddling and bridling.

Newton Douglas with six of his range riders appeared first. The others, he explained, hadn't all had their horses saddled, but they'd be along very shortly.

Claude went back to get his horse. As he led the beast outside, he could hear Jack Mather's bull-bass roar back up by the saloon. If that racket didn't awaken the entire town, nothing else would.

Barney Whitsun and Hank Smith appeared, armed and prepared to ride. Mather eventually got down there on his sorrel mare with the flaxen mane and tail. He had a shapeless old ten-gallon Stetson pulled down almost to his ears as though he'd jammed the hat on as an afterthought.

Altogether there were eight of them. Counting Sheriff Rainey the number was nine. He turned without a word and led them in a lope straight up through town then beyond, and swung off to the left, went almost a hundred yards, and yanked back suddenly to stop. The others piled up behind him, looking perplexed and doubtful.

"Wait right here," he said, and went dashing back down the same alleyway Brion had used to ride out of town, jumped off and charged into his office, snatched up his hat and Clayton's little black notebook, ran back out and sprang again astride his startled horse. When he returned, the posse men were muttering and looking troubled. He still didn't explain everything, as he resumed leadership, but he looped his reins, let his horse walk slowly at its own gait, tipped back his head so as not to lose any of the weak star shine, and opened the black book.

Newton Douglas looked, wrinkled his leathery brow and looked closer. "Claude," he said. "What's wrong with you? If we got to rescue this feller Clayton, believe me, we're never going to do it riding at a walk while you read a damned book."

Claude said nothing. His eyes were flared wide open as he rocked along in the saddle, holding the little book almost against his nose. Finally, with an angry curse, he halted, stepped down, and said: "Jack, hold a match for me so I can see this map."

Mather obeyed, but without the slightest inkling of what any of this was about. He held up seven matches, in fact, before he finally growled at the sheriff: "Claude, you out of your skull?"

Claude lowered the book, looked around, saw the pained, baffled expressions, and started to explain. The longer he talked the more bewildered his posse men became, until, moving right up to the time Brión had abducted Archer Clayton, the entire story began to straighten out and make some kind of sense.

By the time he was finished with his recital, not a man among the vigilantes spoke or took their eyes off Sheriff Rainey. He put the black notebook into his shirt pocket, carefully buttoned down the flap, and reached for the reins of his horse. But he didn't mount up. He simply held the reins in one hand, looking at the others.

"We won't have to try and track them in the moonlight. All we've got to do is set up a real good ambush . . . and wait."

Newton Douglas said: "Wait? Claude, you said he's going to lead this Mexican to the cache. Now the way I see it, from a lifetime of being around Mexicans, when he leads 'em to that gold, they'll shoot him and dump his carcass in the same hole they dig that gold out of."

Claude nodded solemnly. "That's just about the way Brión's figuring to do it, Newt. You're plumb right."

"Then what are we sitting here for?" snapped the cowman.

Claude pointed back toward town with a rigid arm. "Because the lousy cache is in Springville, according to this map. I know every dog-goned landmark on this map, Newt, and that cache is buried down there at the south end of town among those old Mex hovels."

Barney Whitsun gasped and rolled his eyes. "You plumb certain?" he whispered. "You mean to stand there and tell us after all the sweat and struggle we put into making this a decent town to live in . . . all the time there was a damned fortune in gold buried right under our noses we could've used to . . . good Lord!"

Claude turned his horse and began leading it back toward town. The others dutifully turned and followed along in his wake. They spoke a little among themselves in low, incredulous voices. Only Newton Douglas stepped off and strode on up to pace along beside Sheriff Rainey. "Claude," he said gravely, "if you've read that map wrong, you're going to feel almighty bad when we find Clayton's body."

"I've been thinking that," admitted the lawman. "I want a decent light as soon as we reach Mather's saloon to study the map again."

They returned to town like ghosts, wordlessly tied up out front of the Oasis, and then grimly trooped inside. Jack went after a lamp in his storeroom, lighted the thing, and put it down squarely on the bar top where Sheriff Rainey was standing. Then, as Claude took out the black notebook and hunched over it, lips pursed, eyes slitted in hard concentration, Jack began setting up glasses and bottles up and down his bar where the anxious, silent vigilantes leaned and were tensely silent.

Claude eventually reared back, impassively stowed the book a second time, and reached with both hands for a bottle and a glass.

"Well?" demanded Newt Douglas.

"I'm right," Claude growled, and drank off a straight shot of green rye whiskey that made tears spring to his eyes. "Either I'm right or the map's wrong, and Arch Clayton himself drew that map."

A low sigh of sound passed over the crowded bar. Newt ruminated briefly, then said: "Well, boys, Clayton can't stall those Mexicans too long. He'll have to commence leading 'em back to the south end of town pretty soon. Seems to me we ought to start laying plans and drinking less."

Chapter Eleven

They went to the south end of town and when Barney asked Claude where, precisely, the cache was, Claude just gave Barney a sour look.

"What d'you want to know for, ya dog-goned nosy old cuss. Even if I told you, all that'd happen would be a bunch of Mexicans'd come after you for it."

They made a careful study of the *jacales* with Claude leading the way. Someone suggested that they fetch some lanterns. Claude growled at that man, also; if there was one thing they didn't have to do it was let anyone, townsmen or Mexicans either, know that they were down among the *jacales*.

Every one of them was put in the vicinity of some particular *jacal*, either inside it, outside it, on top of it, with strict orders to do nothing at all until Sheriff Rainey gave the orders. After that, with Newton Douglas, Claude sat in the watery-lighted darkness both worried and wearied.

"I figure," he confided to the cowman, "Clayton has got to make out like he's picking up one landmark after another as he leads them back and forth out there stalling for time. I also figure he's hoping like the very devil that I remembered the black notebook and went after it to figure out where he'd have to lead them eventually, once I got loose." He and Newt Douglas exchanged a look. Newt's expression was skeptical so Claude nodded and said: "I know, it's an awful lot of just plain figuring, whereas, if we trailed them, we'd be damned certain. The trouble with that is, Newt, they'd darned well be listening for pursuit and on a quiet night like this one they'd hear us long before we even got close. The second trouble with trailing is . . . on a night as dark as this one you just can't do it with any speed at all."

There could be small doubt but that Sheriff Rainey had chosen the ideal solution to his problem. The question was would it work as it should work?

Newt made a smoke, lit up by ducking around with his head inside the *jacal* at their back, and said it sounded too easy, that old Spanish cache right here in Springville; if it actually was here, how come a feller from as far off as Raton knew about it and no one locally did?

Claude wasn't certain, but he explained how Clayton and his dead partner had evidently stumbled on to a much smaller cache of coins up in the Raton country somewhere that gave the location of this other cache.

Newton Douglas was a hard-headed, hard-working, eminently practical man. He tilted his head, blew smoke, and said: "Y'know, Claude, I been all my life hearing those old tales of buried

Spanish gold, and this is the first time I've ever run across anyone who'd really had any of that stuff in the palm of their hand. Now I'm saying I don't believe . . ."

"Quiet," hissed Claude suddenly, stiffening as he leaned away from their *jacal*, listening to the southward night.

Newt also strained to hear. A full minute passed and Newt heard nothing. He eased back, resumed smoking, and considered the ancient sky. "Probably loose cattle or horses down on the southward range," he muttered. "Claude . . . ? Are you plumb certain this whole thing isn't some kind of hoax and Clayton's in cahoots with the Mexicans to rob Barney's safe of that ten thousand dollars?"

Claude was flabbergasted, initially, but afterward he was scornful. "Newt, I thought *you* of them all would have better sense to pick up a rumor like that and believe it. Why, Clayton's own partner got killed by those Mexicans."

"You only got his word for that, Claude."

"I have like hell. I was standing right there when one of the Mexicans admitted in his dying words this Fernando Bríon had that lad killed."

"Oh, well, you see, I didn't know any of that."

"So," growled Claude, shooting a waspish scowl at his friend, "that makes it easy for you to make wild guesses. *Humph!*"

They stood on, waiting and smoking. Claude

went over in his mind Arch Clayton's map as he now was able to recall it, and felt irritated with himself. *The cache was exactly underneath the mud floor where that Mexican assassin had died.* Why in the devil hadn't he wondered more about why Clayton had stayed down here among the *jacales* rather than up at the hotel?

Well, he consoled himself, it was the old story of hindsight being a heap better than foresight. He flexed his sore arms and studied the position of the moon. It was slightly past midnight according to his calculations. Bríon and Arch Clayton had been gone almost three hours. They'd have covered a lot of country in that length of time.

Big Jack Mather came gliding up soundlessly and said, jutting his chin eastward: "Band of riders coming from the far side of town, Claude. They're moving slow and easy with two men out front. I heard 'em a while back and slipped around for a look. They're beginning to angle off southward like maybe they figure to come into town over the stage road."

Claude told Mather to go back to his position and keep out of sight, then he took Newt with him and passed in and out of the deep, square shadows until they were at the lower extremity of Springville. There, they halted and stood like stone, waiting to pick up the sound of these oncoming strangers.

As it turned out, though, while they heard the horsemen southward, they couldn't see them, and Mather was incorrect at least in one surmise; they didn't turn and enter town from the stage road at all. They walked their horses straight on across the road heading easterly. Newt screwed up his face in deep perplexity but Claude Rainey stood quietly thoughtful. He had an idea what those men might be doing if they were the Mexicans with Clayton. Arch was deliberately see-sawing with his captors out there, bringing them in a little closer with each change of course, so that if Claude was up there waiting, he'd have plenty of warning. In fact, Sheriff Rainey smiled, while his companions stood out there with him, scowling.

He tapped Newt's arm. "Split up," he said quietly. "You take one side while I take the other side. Warn the boys they're coming. Tell them to stay inside those *jacales* for cover and hold off until I give the signal to cut loose. Meet me back up by our hovel, Newt."

The two older men turned at once and started back up through the eerie night where swaying shadows appeared here and there in the Stygian doorways of mud hovels to listen and nod, then step back out of sight again. Barney and Jack Mather, in adjoining *jacales*, listened to Claude carefully, gripped their carbines tighter, and gazed southward where the bland, hot night was still without sound of horsemen.

"You sure?" asked Barney.

Mather growled. "Of course he's sure. I heard 'em myself."

Claude returned to his position and waited for Newton Douglas. In the back of his mind was the very real risk to Arch Clayton. No matter how this turned out, he was confident they'd get the Mexicans, but he was also certain that Fernando Brión, being anything but a dolt, wouldn't permit Clayton to get very far from Brión's gunsight. It would be a miracle, Claude somberly concluded, as Newt strolled up, if Arch Clayton came through this alive.

"All set," stated Douglas, grounding his Winchester and gazing quietly at Sheriff Rainey. "Only one thing sticks in my craw, Claude. Clayton and his chances."

"I know," mumbled the lawman. "I've been thinking on that, too. Maybe, if we held off and gave Brión terms, we could save him."

Douglas shrugged with no more to say. They'd have to improvise as they went along, and while this offered no guarantees, it was the only course available to them. Ten minutes passed. The stillness was so deep it almost had a sound of its own. Claude forced himself to stand and wait, but when another ten minutes had passed and they still heard nothing, his nerves began to crawl. If Brión's horsemen had been coming, they'd most assuredly be close enough by this time for the

120

waiting vigilantes to hear them. Then it struck Claude.

"Hell," he whispered. "They're *on foot*. They left their horses out a ways and are slipping in on foot. Bríon's figured out if there's to be an ambush, it'll be among these dog-goned mud huts." He'd scarcely said that when a man's quick, rising bleat of astonishment rang out, then one solitary gunshot erupted. After that it was a nightmare for Claude Rainey.

No one ever knew who fired that gunshot or made that bleat, but it was afterward considered probable that one of Bríon's men must have stuck his nose inside a *jacal* out of curiosity, saw the vigilante in there with his gun drawn, and tried to cry a warning before he was shot. It was as good a guess as any and immediately after it happened hell broke loose in among the *jacales* where Sheriff Rainey's signal to open up would have also been a gunshot—exactly the sound that had just erupted.

Claude and Newt Douglas, though, were momentarily left out of it. The fight that began raged exclusively over near the east side of the *jacales* not very far into town at all. They went there, slipping back and forth as they advanced.

Gunshots brightened around them each fraction of a second then winked out, leaving the night gloomy again.

The Mexicans were putting up a stiff and

stubborn battle. When Newt Douglas eased around a hovel, two Mexicans blazed away at him immediately. He grimaced and tried again. The second time those gunmen, one eastward, one southward, chipped away big chunks of the adobe wall, making Newt dive back to cover again.

Elsewhere the same furious fighting was in progress. Sheriff Rainey wasn't nearly as interested in shooting Mexicans as he was in locating Archer Clayton. He was very much afraid of what he'd see when he eventually found him, too. Brion would be enraged at what had happened. He'd blame Clayton for it exclusively, Claude felt, and to avoid Clayton's murder—if it hadn't already occurred—he went swiftly back and forth, trying to find some area where Clayton might be.

Someone took a hard hit and screamed. Just for a second that scream attracted enough attention to divert everyone. The gunfire became sporadic and gave Sheriff Rainey enough time to whisk across a little crooked byway and get up near the forefront of the battle. There, when the firing was resumed, he could see where some of the Mexicans had run together into a hovel where they were putting up a fierce fight. Elsewhere, less fortunate invaders were sniping around the corners and from deep in dark shadows.

Rainey's vigilantes had most of the advantage in

this battle although there was no safe way for them to get around the invaders either to capture or kill them. It was, in the vernacular of the Southwest, a Mexican stand-off. Neither side could achieve total triumph.

Jack Mather slipped up behind Claude and said the Mexicans were trying to drop back, were trying to pull back out of town. He wanted to know whether Claude thought they hadn't ought to leave off the fighting and try hard to get out there on the dark plain between Bríon's men and their horses. Claude didn't think so.

"This way we have cover. Out there we'd lose a lot of men. Neither Bríon nor that damned gold is that important to me. By the way, Jack, have you seen where Bríon himself might be? He'll have Clayton with him. We've got to rescue Clayton if we possibly can."

"No sweat on that score, Sheriff," rumbled the big, dark man. "Clayton's up with Barney and Hank in that *jacal* near the north end." At Claude's astonished grunt, Mather explained: "That's what the first shot was about. One of Newt's cowboys saw a Mexican raise his pistol to shoot a white feller they had with 'em, and the cowboy shot first. Clayton dived headfirst into the hovel, and the fight started when a couple of 'em ran after him. Claude, we piled up three dead Mexicans faster'n you could draw a gun."

Claude eased back along the rough mud wall,

looking at Mather. "Which one of Newt's cowboys did that?" he inquired. Mather didn't know which one; all he knew was that it had to be one of Douglas's riders because they were separated from the townsmen before the battle started, and the gunshot came from up where they were.

Claude turned back to gauging the force of combat beyond his shelter. It seemed that Bríon's men were dropping back through the hovels toward the eastward plain, which was the way they'd come into town. He decided it would be fine like that. He had Clayton back alive, and that was, after all, his primary objective. He told Jack to go on around back and pass the word they wouldn't push after the Mexicans beyond the *jacales*.

Later, checking the loads in his six-gun after firing a few rounds at blue-lancing streaks of gun flame, he heard some of the cowboys give a triumphant yell as they ducked back and forth, going in after the Mexicans. He called to them angrily. So did Newton Douglas. The range men then remained where they were, firing and hooting derisively at the withdrawing invaders, catcalling and taunting their enemies.

The fight, savage, deadly, and fiercely prosecuted on both sides as it had been, probably hadn't lasted a full fifteen minutes although to Claude Rainey it seemed to drag on for hours. Newt and his men came over where there were calls for swift pursuit. Claude was dry about that.

"One thing you can say for Mexicans," he told them. "They're some of the best bushwhackers in the world. You boys go charging blind down there now, and they'll drill every damned last one of you. Where's Clayton?"

Arch elbowed through. He and Rainey stood a moment, gazing at one another. "Close," said Claude. "Damned almighty close that time."

Clayton seemed less grim. "Not until we finally got back here to Springville, then I was sweating. There was no way for me to know whether anyone'd even found you in that old shed, let alone have any idea whether you'd figure out from the black notebook where we were going to end up. I reckon, come daylight, I'll have a few gray hairs, Sheriff."

Newt Douglas said: "Claude, they killed two of my men and we've had four wounded."

Rainey nodded. "Get the wounded taken care of, Newt. We'll bury the dead come sunup. How did *they* make out?"

"Five killed an' two inside a *jacal* who couldn't get away, captured."

Claude smiled coldly. "Lead me to the captured ones. I'll lock them up and have a long talk with 'em."

The men turned and began trooping along to where the prisoners were, Sheriff Rainey and Arch Clayton in the lead.

Chapter Twelve

One of the prisoners wasn't more than eighteen years old. That one was terrified. The other one was a man of perhaps forty with the scarred visage, dark and wary eyes of an old, seasoned Mexican guerilla. He was fatalistic. In his own country of Texas, he knew precisely what to expect. A bullet through the head. From the fierce expressions on the faces of Newt Douglas's cowboys he could find ample reason to believe it was also going to happen in Springville, Arizona. When he saw Arch Clayton, he showed surprise, almost astonishment, for by this man's code of existence Clayton should have been among the first to die.

They took the unarmed captives up through town to the jailhouse and locked them in. Afterward, Claude and Arch went with the others to rout the local physician out of bed to care for the wounded. But they found him wide-awake, sitting in a lighted room with all shades drawn, reading a book and waiting. He was caustic when someone murmured surprise.

"Put 'em in there," he said of the wounded, flagging with a hand. Then, looking around into the faces of the others, he said: "What did you expect? You made enough confounded noise down there to awaken the dead. I'd bet you a hundred dollars you couldn't find a household in Springville right now that isn't wide-awake. Just because there are no lights doesn't mean a blessed thing. Now get out of here. I don't need an audience when I work."

It was very late by the time they stopped by Jack Mather's place for a drink, and there Newton Douglas and his men departed for their cow camp leaving Arch Clayton and Sheriff Rainey with only the three or four townsmen including Whitsun, Smith, and Mather.

It took that long for the smokiness to die out of their eyes and the flare of anger from their thoughts. The best way to bring things back to normal perspective was another drink. They all had one. In fact, they all had two more, then Clayton and Claude Rainey headed for the jailhouse, leaving Smith, Whitsun, and Jack Mather in the Oasis to ruminate and relax. It was by then close to 1:00 in the morning.

At the jailhouse Claude brought forth the youngest captive. Without a word Claude took out his six-gun, laid it upon his desk close at hand, sat down, and stonily stared. Arch did the same. He eased down in a chair next to the door, shoved his legs out, tipped down his hat, and looked straight up at the youthful brigand. Over in the big strap-steel cell the older man sat on a bunk, gazing out. He seemed callous and resigned about the younger man's fate.

In Spanish, Claude asked the young *vaquero* three questions. One: would Bríon return to Mexico? Two: had Bríon sent for those other men he'd detached earlier toward Raton? Three: did any of the *vaqueros* know why they were over the line with Mexico?

The youthful captive was pale and big-eyed when he answered. He had no idea where *Don* Fernando would go now, he said. As for the men who had been sent north, *Don* Fernando had already sent for them to return, before the fight. Finally, he said it was rumored secretly among the *vaqueros* that there was a great store of *Gachupin* gold buried in some hidden cache around the town of Springville. It was also said among the *vaqueros* that *Don* Fernando would bring an entire army to Springville if need be to get that cache of gold.

Clayton said: "*Muchacho*, if I opened that door and let you walk out of here . . . where would you go?"

The youth's large dark eyes rolled. "Back to Mexico," he said in tolerable English. "Never more to return to this wild place, Arizona, *señor*. I have always wanted to be in a fine fight before."

"And now, *muchacho*?"

"¡*Ai, caramba*! I was escairt to death, *señor*. I

theenk I be badder to go hoe the maize of my father."

Clayton looked at Claude and raised his eyebrows. Sheriff Rainey nodded, then he said: "Son, take off those silly bandoleers. That's right. Now go on, but remember one thing . . . if either one of us ever so much as sees you this side of the line again . . ." Sheriff Rainey raised a rigid finger and pointed it like a pistol. "*¿Sabe, usted?*"

"*¡Sí, capitán!*" exclaimed the youth. "I understand. Much thanks, *señores*. Much thanks!" He dashed out the door and was almost immediately lost in the yonder darkness. Arch grinned and Sheriff Rainey's tough old eyes briefly glowed, then he strolled over, flung back the cell door, and ordered the tough-faced, older cowboy out.

The routine was almost the same but when they came to the place where they'd released the youth, neither of them made any such offer to the older man. He didn't expect them to, but he said in passable English they were good men to allow the very young a second chance.

"And the older ones?" inquired Claude.

The *vaquero* eloquently shrugged. He wasn't as old as Claude and yet he was older than Arch Clayton. He said: "In some ways, *jefe*, it has been a long life for me." He stood, waiting for the *gringos* to lead him around back into the alleyway.

"Will Bríon come back?" asked Rainey.

The Mexican nodded. "*Sí, señor.* He must come back. There are things you do not know about. He must have that gold. Even though he die, he must try to get it."

Claude caught an inference here he'd failed to meet in the younger captive. "Why so?" he asked.

"*Señor jefe, Don* Fernando is a *pronunciado.* He is going to pronounce himself in revolt against the central government and raise an army. He does not have enough money for this, alone. But with the old Spanish treasure he'd not only be able to raise and equip an army, you understand, but he would also be able to buy some government officials in Mexico City, who would join him in his war against the *presidente.*"

Claude was surprised and showed it. Finally in a very dry tone of voice he said, glancing from the guerilla to Arch Clayton: "That's nice. That lousy gold of yours is going to cause a revolution in Mexico."

Clayton shook his head. "I doubt it, Sheriff. Let's lock this one back up, go get your friends from the saloon, and go dig up that cache and hide it where Brion can't find it."

Sheriff Rainey took the prisoner back, locked him into the cell, returned to stand beside his desk, and asked a question: "Does Brion know where the cache is?"

"You're darned right he knows. How else do you think I stayed alive? He thought I was

130

deliberately trying to lead him back here to town to get massacred. I had to talk like a Dutch uncle, and even draw him a sketch in the dust, before he decided I was too valuable to be killed. He knows all right, and if what old pepper-belly over there in the cell said was the truth, about him financing a revolution, you can damned well be sure Bríon will be back for that cache just as soon as he possibly can."

Clayton stood up, hitched at his shell belt, and went to the door to look up and down the night-darkened roadway. Claude Rainey made a smoke, took one deep-down drag off it, then smashed the thing out on his desk, and put on his hat. He pulled back the door and walked outside, jerked his head when he made certain the lights were still burning up at the saloon, and led the way back up there.

Mather and Barney Whitsun were alone. Hank Smith like all the others had headed for home. Once reaction set in, after just about any fight men fought, there was dogged lethargy. Claude accepted the drink Mather duly poured and downed it, so did Arch Clayton, then the sheriff said: "Well, let's get a lantern, some crowbars and shovels, and go down dig up that cache."

Barney the storekeeper and Mather the saloon man looked shocked, then incredulous, and finally they looked avaricious and began to move. Claude let all their thoughts come and go as a man might who understood exactly how the wheels in the heads of other men would react, then he said: "Get one thing straight. This is not our gold. Jack . . . Barney . . . get that into your skulls. All we're going to do is move the cache so when Bríon comes back all he'll find is an empty hole."

Big Jack Mather's swarthy face fell. He leaned and balefully regarded Claude. "Well, hell," he growled, "if it's not our cache, what're we digging it up for?"

Claude turned vinegary. "Confound it all, Jack, I just told you. So's the Mexicans don't find it when they come back."

Barney shook his head emphatically. "After the shellacking we gave 'em, believe me, Claude, they won't be back."

Claude rolled his eyes in disgust. "Just fetch tools and come along," he said finally. "And just to keep you brought up to date, one of those prisoners we took said Bríon has to come back and make another try for that gold. Now are you coming or do Mister Clayton and I go dig it up by ourselves?"

They came, but more out of sheer curiosity than for any other single reason. It was after 2:00 in the morning when they got to the *jacal*, and even if the stench of burned powder wasn't enough to put their hair on end, no one had bothered moving the Mexicans who'd been killed in the earlier battle. The Arizonans had been carried away, but not Bríon's dead *bandoleros,* and that heightened the discomfort even more.

Claude then detailed Jack to keep watch outside while he and Barney, along with Arch Clayton, took the tools and went inside to dig, and that made them all a little more jumpy.

Arch lit the lantern, stepped over near the identical spot where the Mexican cowboy had cashed in, and stamped his foot several times, then slammed a crowbar into the ground and started levering up flat, hard layers of packed earth.

For the most part they dug in grim silence. Once Barney paused to wipe off sweat and swear there was nothing where they were digging but fifty miles of hardpan and on the other end of that a whole herd of queued-up Chinamen. Claude took over to give Barney a rest and later Barney went out to take the sentry chore over and big Jack Mather came in to also dig. It was Mather who was using the crowbar when they reached the cache. It was four feet down and covered with ancient rotted fir planks. Barney forgot to watch outside when he heard the others exclaim over the discovery. They all crowded up to help Jack and Arch boost the lead-coated oaken box out of the ground.

"Heavy . . . as . . . hell," gasped mighty Jack Mather, giving the final heave. "If that's all gold in the box, then there's enough there to make us all rich."

They grunted the box over near the lantern. Claude looked up, saw Barney standing in the doorway watching, and snarled at him. "You keep watch out there, Barney. That bunch of Mexes could sneak back here and jump the lot of us."

Barney turned reluctantly and resumed his position outside. Claude straightened up and put both hands low upon his own back. Digging that deep, that hard, was a kind of manual labor he'd been sedulously avoiding for thirty years. "Let's take it up to the jailhouse," he said, grimacing from the pain in his back.

It took all of them, including Barney, to hoist the oaken old rotting box and stagger outside with it. The moon was gone and the star shine was weak and watery. They had to pause three times and finally Claude's back gave out entirely so he traded places with Barney Whitsun, walking behind them keeping close watch in all directions. Barney grunted and staggered until they were almost up to his store, then he called a halt and said: "Mister Clayton, since this is your cache, what say we take it into my back room and open the box, then store the gold in my safe along with that ten thousand dollars?"

Clayton was willing. Like the others he was exhausted; this had been a long, tumultuous night. Before he answered though, he glanced over at Sheriff Rainey. Claude shrugged. He said he didn't give a damn where they took the box as long as they got it off the sidewalk and some-where out of sight.

Barney unlocked his front door, grunted with the others the full length of his store through pitch darkness, and led them into a musty old room with laden shelves where they finally stopped, dropped the box, and stood around in strong silence just looking at it.

"Get a pinch bar," said Claude, setting up their lantern and bending to light the thing. "And, Barney, take a look up and down the front roadway just in case, will you?"

While Whitsun was gone, Arch kneeled and examined the huge old hand-made steel lock as well as the massive hasp that held it secured to the oaken box. "It's going to take a right stout pinch bar," he commented, then resumed his standing position.

Jack Mather leaned upon a wall, gazing upon the box. He clearly was running hot and cold to see the interior of the thing. When Barney returned, Jack sprang forward to take the pinch bar and sink down on both knees beside the box. The others crowded up close. Claude said: "Barney, see anyone out there?" Whitsun shook his head without looking up as Jack set the pinch bar and began to heave his considerable heft against it to pry loose the hasp, then he looked around.

"We got to shoot the lock off," he panted.

"Claude, this here hasp is bolted through the oak."

Sheriff Rainey shook his head. "Shooting will make too much noise. Keep worrying at it, Jack."

Mather resumed his prying, but at Arch Clayton's suggestion shifted to a corner of the lid, and that achieved success because the lid was punky with wet rot. With a ripping sound it broke, revealing part of the interior of the box. Dull coins darkly glistened, and with Mather savagely attacking the rotten wood, the smooth end of several bars of gold bullion also showed.

No one said a word until Mather, panting hard, rocked on his haunches and dropped the pinch bar, then Barney, bending stiffly, said: "Good . . . Lord!"

Claude looked. So did Arch Clayton who owned this treasure. Claude's voice was unchanged when he said: "Well, Bríon had reason to spill blood. I reckon a lot of men have died for a lot less."

They bent to lift out the treasure and lay it reverently on the floor. The gold coins came from four broken old rotted doeskin bags. There had been two of those bags on each end of the box, probably packed like that to prevent the six bars of smelted-down, pure gold from shifting or loosening inside.

When it was all laid out, Jack Mather mopped off sweat and looked pale. So did Barney Whitsun. Claude Rainey made a smoke, eyed the fortune caustically, and shot a sidelong glance at the owner of all that wealth.

Arch rocked back on his heels, solemn as an owl. In an almost funereal voice he said: "I'll tell you honestly, men, I wouldn't have traded it for the life of my partner. I wouldn't even have wanted to keep it for the life of that Mexican bushwhacker I shot down below the line and fetched back up here with me." He stood up, looked at them, and removed his hat to drag a soiled sleeve across his forehead. "Right now it sort of makes me sick, just thinking all the grief I've seen over getting it, and that's not mentioning the blood and anguish the Indians put out, to work it down for those old-time Spaniards."

Claude Rainey exhaled a big cloud of smoke, looked at the burly, younger man, and quietly said: "Arch, there's nothing wrong with gold or money. There never has been. It's just the way folks have been using it, that's wrong." He held out his tobacco sack but Clayton shook his head.

"Mister Whitsun," he said, "let's stow this stuff in your safe out of sight before someone else gets shot over it."

They solemnly bent to this new task. It took a half hour and afterward, trooping outside to the night, they were surprised to find that their grim and ghostly world had brightened toward dawn in their absence.

Chapter Thirteen

Barney, Jack, and Sheriff Rainey were dog tired. Arch Clayton was also weary, but he was in a kind of shock. They had tried, each in his own way by his own measures and values, to estimate the value of that golden hoard. The lowest figure was so high Arch Clayton had felt breathless. Now, when the others said they had to head for their beds, he struck out for the café across the road that was just opening for the new day's business.

Claude watched him cross the road and gave his head a little caustic shake. Claude couldn't rightfully say he knew how Clayton felt, but he had some idea of the weight of the responsibility the younger man was carrying. Claude turned and headed for his room at the hotel. If Brión was coming back, it wouldn't be for a while yet— perhaps not even for several days or a week, because there were no more guerillas this side of the line.

Claude stopped in mid-stride. No? Like hell there weren't. The only difference was that Brión would have to pay a high price for them, and they wouldn't be the color of old shoe leather, but in Arizona, if Fernando Brión chose to do it that way, he could hire all the professional gunfighters and killers he'd need. He wouldn't have to go any farther than the border towns to find men like that.

In fact, Claude thought, standing on the landing of the rooming house, if Brían got the idea as it had just struck Claude himself, Brían could have his hired murderers and be back in Springville by tomorrow night.

He started climbing again toward his upstairs room. *Tomorrow* night. That still gave him most of today and all of tonight to get caught up on his rest.

It was unusual, going to bed just as others arose, but Claude had been there before; it did not appreciably trouble him. Once, as he gazed out the window and down into Springville's main roadway, he saw the queues of curious, questioning people and realized that the entire town was full of sensible curiosity about the fight last night. He was glad he was in his room.

He slept soundly until 2:00 in the afternoon when someone came to peck diffidently on his door. He called out asking who it was. Hank Smith, the blacksmith answered. Claude groaned under his breath, rolled out, tugged on his breeches, boots, stood up to shrug into his shirt, then he reached for his six-gun, and finally went over to open up and confront Smith.

Hank was a durable, muscular man with a serious manner. He very rarely smiled and never laughed aloud. He wasn't laughing or smiling now, either. He was looking very solemn.

"Newt Douglas sent a man in looking for you. When he couldn't find you at Jack's place nor at the jailhouse, he come up to my shop. Claude, Newt's sighted a band of men heading for Springville over the southeasterly desert."

Sheriff Rainey was nonplussed. "Brion . . . ?" he whispered.

Hank nodded. "Newt's cowboy says if it ain't Brion, then it's got to be some other kind of trouble from below the line because Newt told 'em at their cow camp the approaching men are armed to the teeth and ready for war."

"All right," murmured the lawman, turning back into his room. "Much obliged, Hank. Much obliged. I'll come down as soon as I've finished dressing."

It took him a half hour. He had two days' growth of whisker stubble to shear off, and he also had to get all the cobwebs out of his brain with a vigorous washing. Then, when he walked out into the afternoon sunlight, three men saw him and converged like hungry hawks. Barney Whitsun reached him first. "Claude," he said. "We got to get shed of that damned treasure out of my safe. I was up at Jack's place when Newt Douglas's cowboy was sipping a beer and talking. I know who's coming and I also know why, and, Claude, if he thinks the gold's in my safe, he could fire the whole blessed building. We've got to . . ."

"If you could hear yourself, Barney, you'd be ashamed," Rainey said, looking at Jack Mather and Arch Clayton. Elsewhere, up and down the roadway, men were coming together here and there, somber and careful with their talk. Evidently that cowboy of Newton Douglas's had spread the word very effectively. Claude wished he could have been at the Oasis when the range man was doing that; he'd have run him out of town with his ears ringing.

"Anybody called the vigilantes together again?" he asked, looking straight at swarthy Jack Mather, the saloon man.

Jack scowled and shook his head. "Been waiting for you to show up," he muttered.

With great forbearance Claude nodded and said: "All right, Jack, I've showed up. Now send out word for 'em to gather at your place . . . and fast . . . because if Newt Douglas's man saw those Mexicans this morning coming across the south range, they could reach Springville by milking time without having to hurry at all."

Arch Clayton waited until Jack was briskly walking away, then he said if Claude thought it best, he'd move his cache out of Barney's safe and hide it somewhere else. Claude was caustic about that.

"Where, my friend? Just where could you lug

that big a bunch of booty in broad daylight without half the town seeing you at it? And just where could you hide it? Back in the same danged hole we dug it out of last night?" Claude didn't give Clayton an opportunity to answer any of those questions. He turned on sweating Barney Whitsun with an unpleasant expression and said: "Well . . . ?"

Barney withered. "All right, leave it there. But, Claude, they'll find out sure as hell, and you know that. Somehow they're going to find out where that blasted stuff is."

Claude's caustic manner lingered. "That's what Brion's returning for, isn't it? Well, then, of course he'll find out. Barney, sometimes I wonder about you. That man has sacrificed a half dozen lives already to get at that cache. You're damned right he's going to find out it's been moved, and he'll undoubtedly hear where we put it, too. Our problem's not trying to keep all that quiet, our problem's keeping him from getting it."

Claude took Arch Clayton with him across to the jailhouse where he contemplated his hungry prisoner and was in turn regarded steadily by the black-eyed Mexican. The man was smoking a brown-paper cigarette. He gravely inclined his head and said: "Good morning, *señores*."

They nodded. Sheriff Rainey asked if the Mexican was hungry. He retorted that he was,

142

indeed, very hungry, but if the *jefe* was too busy he could wait.

Claude picked up his booted carbine, gave his head a hard shake, and went back outside. He said something uncomplimentary about the Mexican, and led the way to the café where, from the door-way, he left word for the man to be fed, then he and Arch walked on down to the livery barn without Sheriff Rainey explaining what he had in mind until he'd growled at the lazy day man to fetch their horses.

"I'm not doubting Newton Douglas's man," he said, "but I want to see Bríon's new crew for myself."

The way Claude said that made it sound as though he were skeptical regardless of the dis-avowal, but Arch Clayton was shrewd enough to see through Sheriff Rainey's remark and say: "I've been wondering a little myself, Sheriff."

Claude looked round. "Wondering about what?"

"If he has more Mexicans with him, or another kind of gunfighter."

Claude puckered his eyes at their outer corners in a critical little squint. "You're going to get by in this life just fine," he said gruffly. "All you've got to do is keep both eyes open like you're doing now, and stop finding hidden darned caches of other folks' gold."

They left town by going southward, then east-ward, and around upon the yonder desert where not many townsmen would see them riding out. As Sheriff Rainey said, the town'd had enough upset stomachs for one night and day, no point in making the ailment chronic.

They headed in the general direction of Dead Man's Cañon. "For some reason I don't exactly understand," said Claude, "that seems to be the area everyone makes for lately."

"Not any more it won't be," contradicted Clayton. "Before, probably because my partner tried to bury the box of cash there before he was shot down, Bríon's men must have figured the rest of the cache was buried thereabouts somewhere. But you can bet on it, Sheriff, he knows a damned sight better now."

"Mebbe," muttered Sheriff Rainey, and kept right on riding toward Dead Man's Cañon through the blue-blurred, smoky heat waves, as though this kind of full-force, dehydrating summertime scald didn't really bother him very much at all.

They came around upon the far northward plateau above Dead Man's Cañon and for the second time left their animals a fair distance to the rear, took their carbines, and crept up where they could lie belly-down upon the hot soil like a pair of skulking Apaches, and slit their eyes for a slow, meticulous, and long study of the empty world all around.

Heat rolled up out of the cañon, writhed in the air, and bore with it a scent that was partly stale, partly metallic. The men sweated hard, their clothing darkened, and still they saw neither horsemen nor the dust that inevitably arose beneath the hoofs of horsemen in this powder dry, musty country. Sheriff Rainey was dogged about it.

Arch said: "They'll come in from the south, if he's got *gringos* with him, Sheriff, and they'll split up so his new hirelings can drift into town maybe one and two at a time. We're likely to lie here all day today and all day tomorrow and still not see anything. Besides that, I'm thirsty."

"Stick a pebble under your tongue," grunted Claude, and kept to his vigil.

But in the end Rainey had to admit Arch could be right, for obviously no one was coming up the broad trough of Dead Man's Cañon. They went back to their drowsing horses, got aboard, and turned back. It was then midafternoon with the brassy, faded yellow sun slipping down a pale sky toward some smoking rims far to the west.

When they were in sight of town again, Arch said: "Split up, Sheriff. You come in from the north. I'll ride around and come in from the south. You've the badge. They'll spot you right off. Me, I'm just another sweaty cowboy . . . unless Bríon happens to be along to point me out to them."

"Humph," growled Claude, "Bríon's not that stupid." Arch loped away, heading down across the range on an angling course that would bring

him into Springville down where the livery barn stood. Across the wide old dusty roadway from the barn, and meandering still farther southward, was that abandoned, gloomy clutch of ancient *jacales.*

Sheriff Rainey entered town, as agreed, from the north. He hadn't felt particularly thirsty until he got far enough along to see the Oasis, Jack Mather's place, then, pondering the certainty of cool beer in there, thirst began to torment him. Still, he didn't turn in, although he noticed several horses at the tie rack out front. Instead, he poked along, heading for the livery barn to see that his mount was watered and fed first. He expected to meet Arch down there, but when he rode in Clayton was nowhere around, although his horse was in its stall comfortably eating at the manger.

The sweating hostler came dragging up to take Claude's animal and wordlessly lead it away. A dozen or so big blue-tailed flies aimlessly buzzed in slow, shallow circles, lethargic enough for a man to massacre every one of them with one hard swipe with his hat.

The town seemed quiet. So far, no one had hustled up to inquire of the sheriff the meaning of all that gunfire the night before, but then he hadn't been around very much, so he wryly thought others such as Barney and Jack had had to make the explanations, and if that were so, he told himself as he started up the east side of the roadway toward Mather's saloon, he could imagine what kind of lurid rumors were abroad by this late afternoon time of day.

He had no inkling of trouble at all, wasn't even thinking of violence, when a stranger stepped off the plank walk over in front of his jailhouse, walked twenty feet onto the road, and called: "Lawman! This is it!"

Claude was taken completely by surprise, and that was ordinarily fatal, as that gunman apparently knew very well when he yelled his challenge, because he then went for his gun. Claude not only had to gather his wits, he also had to twist his body and go for his gun all at the same time. But before he could complete his draw another man stepped from a doorway, yelled, and fired. The travel-stained stranger was caught hard by that slug and knocked down. He twisted, as did Claude, and saw Arch Clayton—too late. He collapsed, his unfired gun sliding out into hot roadway dust.

Claude had his gun up and cocked. For five seconds he looked from Clayton to the dead man then back again, before walking out to take a closer look at the corpse. Clayton came only as far as the edge of the plank walk. He looked slowly up and down the road, then punched out the spent casing, plugged in a fresh load, and dropped his six-gun into its holster.

"I saw them setting it up," he said into the

deathly silence as people moved out to crane down toward the sheriff and the dead man at his feet. "Good thing we split up, Sheriff."

Claude stepped across the body and walked on over. "Who's them?" he asked, halting in front of Clayton.

Arch jerked a thumb. "The others are over at the Oasis. Four of them were at a table including this one. If you want, we can go arrest the other three right now."

Claude's bushy brows lifted, his eyes puckered. "Bríon . . . ?"

Clayton shrugged. "I don't know who else, do you?"

Claude turned without answering, gazed back where men were beginning to cluster around the dead man out in the roadway, then let all his pent up breath out in a long sigh. "No," he said, "I don't know who else'd be behind it." He lifted his shoulders. "All right, son, let's go get the other three."

They started across the roadway on a diagonal course heading toward the Oasis. People watched, drawing back, from the looks on their faces. There was a lot of bafflement in Springville about events lately, but one thing was clear enough—Clayton and Sheriff Rainey had *that look* on their faces, so now wouldn't be a very good time to accost either of them for answers to questions.

Chapter Fourteen

Jack Mather was waiting in his doorway with a cluster of local range men and townsmen around him. "They're gone," gasped Jack, still badly shaken by what had come within a hair's breadth of being the end of Claude Rainey. "When one of 'em saw Arch kill their friend out there in the roadway, he run over, said something, and the three of 'em ran out my back door into the alleyway."

Claude went through to look, but there was no sign of anyone out back. When he returned, Arch was waiting for him at the bar, grim-lipped and bleak-looking. Cowmen were pushing up all around, but Arch was ignoring them.

Old Newt Douglas came walking in looking smoky-eyed and high-headed. When he spotted Claude and Arch, he strode on over, slapped his hat down atop the bar, and growled at Mather for drinks. Douglas then turned, looked down his long nose in a sternly reproving manner at the men clustering around, and when these began to wander off, Newt said: "I don't understand, Claude, why you?"

"That's not so hard to understand," stated Clayton. "With the law out of the way, Bríon's new variety of killers would pretty much have things their own way in Springville. But they aren't after the sheriff."

Claude nodded without commenting, and when his drink came, he dropped it straight down and thumped the bar with the empty glass for a refill. Finally he said: "Arch, let's take a walk down and look in that blasted hole we dug last night."

Arch was surprised. "What for?"

Claude shrugged and turned to go. Clayton at once also departed, and moments later, not comprehending exactly, Newt Douglas ambled along in their wake with three of his hard-eyed range riders.

When they reached that place in the road where the killing had occurred not long before, the body was gone, and shortly thereafter, passing Barney Whitsun's front door, the physician they'd taken Newt Douglas's men to the previous night after the fight at the lower end of town, stepped forth and nearly collided with Sheriff Rainey.

The doctor recovered at once, eyed Claude with total equanimity, and held up a package he was carrying. "Formaldehyde," he said dryly. "Do you want the dead Mexicans embalmed, too, Sheriff? The cost will be an extra two dollars per corpse."

Claude glared, stepped around and went on again. Near the lower end of town, he said under his breath: "Someday I'm going to punch him right on the nose. He always acts like *I* make these things happen."

They also found that the dead *vaqueros* had been carted off, which was evidently what had prompted the physician's gallows humor.

Inside the old *jacal* they went up to the excavation and looked in. While they were at it, the liveryman strolled over to look with astonishment at the neat hole and scratch his head as he said: "It sort of got my curiosity up, seeing folks slipping in and out over here so I figured I'd have a look for myself. Sheriff, for a grave it's near deep enough, but ain't it a mite short?"

Claude looked at Arch Clayton. "This is how lies get spread," he said, and turned away without explaining, went back to the doorway, and faced the room from there, fixing the puzzled liveryman with a cold and piercing look.

"Who else was over here today?" he growled.

"Well, I dunno exactly," came the liveryman's reply. "It was just some fellers on horseback. They went poking and looking into five or six of these old mud houses, then when they come to this one, they spent a little more time here than at the other places. Then they mounted up and rode off again."

"How many?" asked Claude.

"Four, Sheriff. Strangers to me. Tough-looking crew, too, if you was to ask."

"And after they left here, they rode north up the roadway toward Jack's saloon?"

The liveryman nodded, cast another puzzled look down into what he thought was a mighty short grave, and wandered back outside, heading toward his place of business.

Clayton, strolling outside, too, said: "Well, there are only three of them now, Sheriff, but I reckon there wouldn't even have to be that many, would there?"

"Nope, son, there sure wouldn't. It'd only take one man to head out where Bríon's hiding and tell him there's a hole in the floor of this *jacal*."

"And," said Newton Douglas, joining the other two outside, "the fireworks will start."

They went back up toward the café. Men, and women also, turned to gaze after them as they strode past. That made Claude vinegary again. He said to Arch Clayton: "Son, you're going to be famous as the man who killed a gunfighter to save my life."

"He'll be doing right good, Claude," put in Douglas, "if he manages to save his own life, after this." When the other two halted outside the café, Douglas shook his head and said: "I'll be up at the Oasis when you're finished. I'll pass the word we might have visitors tonight. All right, Claude?"

"Good idea, Newt."

Archer Clayton and the sheriff ate in dogged

silence. There were only two other patrons in the place, and they were at tables across the room nowhere near the counter, so Claude could speak normally when he said: "He can't try that again and he knows it. That doesn't leave him a whale of a lot of room for maneuvering."

Clayton thought otherwise. "It leaves him plenty of ground, Sheriff, and for ambushing folks right in town, he's got the best friend of all. It'll be dark directly."

They left the café, went down to see how the prisoner was making out, and found the Mexican sitting like an Indian, both legs crossed under him, on his wall bunk. He was briefly impassive and silent, but when the *gringos* turned their backs on him he arose, leaned upon the bars, and asked in a quietly dignified and diffident way what had happened when he'd heard gunshots a while back.

"Your boss lost another gunfighter," said Claude gruffly. "Only this time he wasn't a Mex, he was a border gunman from our side of the line. That satisfy you, *amigo*?"

The Mexican broadly grinned. "It satisfies me very much," he said in Spanish. "But I think, *jefe*, you can't kill them all, and he will keep on sending them until sooner or later . . ."

"Yeah," growled Claude. "Go back to sleep, Pancho."

They had a smoke, privately reflecting upon

what the prisoner had just said. He was perfectly right; sooner or later, since Claude, even with Arch Clayton's help, couldn't shoot them down as fast as Fernando Brión could hire them and send them into Springville to get the sheriff, there was going to be a vacancy in the legal department of Apache County.

Claude fished out the U.S. deputy marshal's badge Arch had left with him earlier, and tossed it over to the younger man. "Wear it or pocket it," he said. "It won't make much difference. Brión knows you well enough by sight, and that badge isn't going to make him harder to live with or easier, either, for that matter, where you're concerned."

Barney Whitsun walked in with sweat dripping and with his holstered six-gun belted low. "The fellers are wondering," he said to Claude Rainey. "What do we do now . . . just wait?"

Claude gazed upon the merchant with softening features. "I reckon that's about the size of it, Barney. You want to remember that if we boil out of town, even with thirty or forty men, we probably wouldn't see anything but their dust, and we just might be doing exactly what he's hoping we'll do, so he can storm into Springville, shoot every fourth or fifth person, dynamite your safe, and make off with the cache."

Whitsun took it differently when Sheriff Rainey laid it out cold for him like that, than either

154

Claude or Arch would have thought. He merely signified understanding with one bird-like inclination of his head, then started out as he said: "We'll be up there waiting. Newt's keeping his men in town and Jack's rounding up a few more willing souls because we figured it out. Brion's still got about fifteen of his Mexicans, as well as them three gunslingers, and that makes a right sizeable army for these parts."

Arch grinned when Barney was gone. Claude came very close to grinning back. He thumbed back his hat and said: "Not the bravest in the world, but brave enough."

Arch thought a moment, then said: "It's a solid town, Sheriff. Solid enough folks. That ten thousand lying over there in his safe, Sheriff, I'll donate. It cost the best friend a man ever had in his life. Whatever you do with it, do it in my partner's name. All right?"

Claude said that was fine with him. He then explained about the white-painted schoolhouse he'd had in the back of his mind, and all the while the black, fatalistic eyes of their Mexican prisoner looked out at them. Finally the Mexican said: "*Señores*, I would like the answer to only one question . . . do you hang me or shoot me?"

Claude turned, stonily regarded the prisoner for a moment before answering, then said: "Not enough evidence against you, *paisano*, to do either, I reckon. But unless you're almighty lucky, you'll sure be gray as a badger before you get out of prison. This isn't Mexico. We don't make you turn your back then blow the top out of your skull."

The prisoner said without so much as the flicker of an eyelash: "*Gracias* . . . thank you . . . *señores*. There are many times in a man's life when he is ashamed of himself. For me, this is one of them. I have been in here thinking. It is not very often a man's solitary memories make him like himself any the better. Today and last night I don't like myself at all."

"What's this all about?" asked Arch Clayton. "You a preacher of some kind down around Rosario?"

The Mexican looked momentarily astonished, then he broke into a huge grin of appreciation of some vastly private joke. "Far from that, *caballeros*," he retorted in soft Spanish. "I have been many things, mostly a guerilla soldier for my *patrón*, but there are two things I've never been, a priest or a murderer."

"That might help a little at your trial," said Claude, and started to turn his back. The Mexican began speaking again, to hold Sheriff Rainey's attention.

"*Don* Fernando will attack this town, *señor*."

"How do you know that?" Claude demanded.

"*Señor*, I know my *patrón*. I've been with him in a hundred raids. I know how he thinks and

156

what he is waiting for right this minute. True, he will hire *gringos pistoleros* such as the one you killed outside this afternoon, but that will only be to while away the time in small things to keep busy. He will sit out there in his camp and send Mexican *vaqueros* back down by Rosario to round up all his retainers. Then he will come into your town like a scourge . . . like a whirlwind . . . *Señor Jefe*. He will kill and burn and pillage. And believe me for what I say is the very truth, *señores* . . . he will get that gold."

Very gradually Claude eased back in his chair, staring hard over at his prisoner. He didn't say a word for a long while, but eventually, as Arch Clayton stood up and gazed out into the shadowy roadway, mantled now by the shades of dusk, he said, speaking Spanish as the prisoner had also done: "We'll see, *vaquero*, we will see how your fine *Don* Fernando Bríon comes out, if he tries that. This is Springville, not Rosario or some other Mexican village."

The prisoner shrugged. "A man can only do so much from behind bars, *jefe*. I have warned you. It is all I can do for you." He turned, went back to his bunk, and sat down again.

Clayton stood in the doorway, looking thoughtful. Up the road near the Oasis some riders were dismounting out in the roadway. At the opposite end of town, the liveryman was standing on a rickety box, touching fire to the wicks in his doorside lamps. Otherwise, Springville was readying itself for the end of another day. "Sheriff," Clayton said without looking around into the office, "he's had since yesterday, providing he really did send south for more *vaqueros*. And providing they'll come . . . which I reckon they will, if he hints at a bonus in gold . . . they ought to be heading right up Dead Man's Cañon about now."

"Providing," growled Sheriff Rainey, getting to his feet, giving his hat brim a hard tug downward, "he's ready, he just might attack tonight, is that what you're saying?"

"That's it, Sheriff, in a nutshell."

Rainey walked out, locked his jailhouse door from the outside, and considered the empty, quiet roadway all around. "Suppertime," he murmured. "I wish I was standing here tomorrow night instead of tonight, Archer. Then I'd know I'd have lived through it. Well, hell, let's amble on up to the Oasis, hoist a couple, and spread the glad tidings. Nothing like glad tidings to keep fellows wide-awake on a night like this one's going to be."

Chapter Fifteen

Claude had an idea and acted upon it without consulting Clayton or anyone else, as was his natural way. He sent one of Newt Douglas's men southeastward over to the heights looking down into Dead Man's Cañon, with instructions to spy on anyone over there, but not to let them see him, and under no circumstances to try and wage any one-man war.

After that he told the hushed men in Mather's saloon what he thought might happen this night. He also told them why he considered it likely.

"That Mex prisoner we've got is having little prickles of conscience for some reason, maybe because I told him he'd be tried in court instead of taken out in the alley and shot, the way he'd have done to any of us if positions were reversed. Anyway, he says Bríon'll attack Springville as soon as his cowboys show up, and I'd say we'd be foolish not to take heed."

Barney Whitsun, sitting at a table, squirmed on his chair. He perhaps had most to lose if a real fight developed—not just his life, but his inventory as well. But Barney said nothing.

There were fifteen of them, mostly range men, but with a few townsmen, too, like Barney and Mather and Hank Smith, the horse-shoer. They had drinks and talked among themselves, now and then calling a question over to Claude or Arch Clayton who stood at the bar glumly with Newton Douglas. There was plenty of resolve, particularly in the range men whose very existence was built around crises and violence.

Newt's cowboy didn't return to town until well after dark. His news was electrifying, and again the Oasis, usually both noisy and full of shifting movement, turned very still and very silent.

"They wasn't in the cañon," related the spy. "They was out of it to the northwest. But all the same that's the way they come, right up Dead Man's Cañon."

"How many?" asked the cowboy's employer.

"Fair sized mob of 'em, Newt. I'd guess 'em to number maybe twenty men."

"Was Bríon with 'em?"

"Not that I could see, and I particular watched for that fancy saddle of his. Nope, these were fresh ones, all Mexicans, all rigged out for war. They even had a couple scouts out front. 'Course. I come in behind 'em."

For ten seconds no one said anything. Mather set up a free drink for the scout and leaned heavily across his bar eyeing Claude Rainey. "Twenty more," he murmured in that deep-down voice of his. "Claude, by my calculations that gives Bríon just about forty men, counting his Yankee gunslingers."

"I can add," growled the sheriff, and faced the room. "We're going to need twice as many men as we've got," he told the others in a strong voice. "I don't figure there'd be much sense in trying to raise that many from the outlying ranches. Sending maybe five or ten of you out to fetch 'em to town would only weaken us here, and in the meantime, while you boys were gone, Bríon might come. So, we'll have to round 'em up right here in town." He gestured toward the door. "Spread out, boys, see what you can come up with. Get 'em from their supper tables or out of bed, but get 'em!"

Barney Whitsun added his two-bits' worth to that. "You can tell them this here is their town, too. If those Mexicans take this place, their women and kids'll suffer, and more'n likely they'll have their houses and stores burned down around 'em."

There was a raw, grating sound as men pushed back chairs to arise and wordlessly, gravely stamp on out of the saloon. Only three or four remained. Claude rapped the bar top and Jack went for a bottle and some glasses that he set up where Newt, Arch, and Claude Rainey were standing. He poured them all drinks and then one for himself. He half lifted his glass and said: "Here's to hell, boys, may the stay there be as pleasant as the way there."

No one smiled.

Newton Douglas asked what Claude was

thinking, and the lawman gave his answer bluntly. "If we had enough men to run that devil down, I'd be for hitting him before he hit us. I'd a sight rather peck at him beyond Springville than let him get in among the buildings and maybe set a fire."

Clayton and Douglas thought on that. Eventually Clayton said: "He won't figure there are more than maybe fifteen of us, Claude, so if we detached maybe ten men to make it look like they were a posse out hunting him. . . ."

"You can't hoodwink that one," muttered Rainey. "He'd by-pass the decoys and still hit the town."

"Agreed," exclaimed Arch calmly. "That's exactly the point. The rest of us would be watching for him, and waiting, with guns and plenty of shells." Clayton paused to lend emphasis to his final sentence. "Stop him cold before he reached town, out on the range."

Claude considered the bottom of his shot glass with squinted eyes. He turned the glass in one rough fist, then put it down very gently, and pushed it away as he straightened back to shoot a wondering look up at Arch. "It's a fair notion," he conceded. "What d'you think, Newt?"

"Sure worth a try, Claude. Otherwise, we got to sit here and wait, got to let Bríon make the first move, and that's never too good in a mess like this."

Mather was nodding in agreement even though

162

no one had asked him for an opinion. The road-side doors flew open and seven men walked in, two of them cowboys, the other five sleepy-eyed, armed townsmen. Mather boomed a relieved welcome and offered free drinks on the house. The new-comers dutifully filed on up.

Ten minutes later another little band of townsmen walked in, also armed but seeming drowsy. This time Barney Whitsun and Hank Smith were accompanying them. After that, an almost steady stream of men filed into Mather's saloon. The place began to resemble some secret rendezvous of brigands there were so many guns in evidence. Not just carbines and six-guns, but even rifles and shotguns.

Clayton smiled. "Close to thirty men already," he told Claude and Newt, "and they're still coming."

It was true. Before the last bunch entered the place the number had risen almost to forty. Eventually, there were close to fifty armed, whisker-stubbled, grim-faced men congregated. Claude's eyes brightened from despair and dogged dourness to grim pleasure. Barney and Hank talked loudly, explaining what was happening. Now and then Jack Mather's deep voice rumbled a resolute oath or a grisly promise.

Claude went among them, selecting ten men for the pseudo posse. In absolute silence he explained what these men were to do. "Ride northward for a few miles up the stage road like you're seeking sign of 'em. Then swing westerly . . . but be damned careful after you leave the road. The idea's not for you to find 'em, but for them to find you. Don't make any armed contact if you can prevent it. There's enough moonlight for them to figure you're a posse being led by me, which is exactly what we want 'em to think so they'll slip around you and head straight for town." Claude smiled broadly, the first such expression Arch Clayton had ever seen him display. "After you've made a big enough sashay around the countryside to be pretty sure you've been spotted, ride easterly until you're darned sure you're far enough over there, then cut southward and come back into town from down below. By then Brión ought to be attacking. If he is, you'll sure as hell hear the shooting." He looked at them. "You boys understand?"

They understood and mumbled to that effect, then Claude sent them on their way to get mounted and head out. He and Arch and Newt Douglas strolled outside to watch those men gather together in the roadway and silently lope up the roadway out of Springville. Afterward, returning to the saloon, the three of them laid their plans for the defense of their town. Newt was to take some of the men and string them out east and south. Claude would take more men and string them along the outskirts from west to south. Arch Clayton was to take the remaining men and cover the north end of town. This, Claude thought, would cover Springville completely and all round. If any one large body of riders was sighted, the men were to challenge once, then open fire on them.

Mather shed his apron and took up his carbine from its corner. When he reached for the lamp, though, Claude told him to leave it burning. He then led the exodus out the back way and Jack's saloon quietly emptied of customers.

That thickening little old moon was up there riding as serenely as always. It was a clear mid-summer night with all the stars turned blue from the dust in the air. There wasn't a breeze stirring anywhere, but all the soft scents of the desert were in the atmosphere around them, and the warmth was pleasant for a change.

Newt took his part of their men and struck out with them. Claude lingered a little longer, going over in his mind anything that might occur for which he'd made no provision. Arch, sensing what was keeping the sheriff, said: "There are no guarantees, it's like riding a green colt. You figure you know everything he'll do, and you take all the precautions, but beyond that you sort of have to meet each emergency just like you'd never met it before. Good luck, Sheriff."

Claude nodded, still pensive, called some

names, and took his men around to the main roadway and on across into the darkness around the buildings and homes on the west side of town. There, he detailed the most reliable men to string out southward until they met some of Newt's men. After that he slipped away and hastened on up through the alleyway gloom to make certain Arch Clayton was in his place.

Arch was—at least he was aligning his men across the upper end of town so they'd make contact on both ends of their strung-out line, with the others.

Claude had a strong hunch Bríon would come out of the northwest. He didn't have much factual reason to expect this beyond a feeling that Bríon would be up there somewhere, since that particular part of the desert was especially empty and untraveled, plus the fact that riders arriving in the Springville country who'd traversed Dead Man's Cañon would find this their easiest route of access.

He returned along the westerly side of town and at once was hailed by two disheveled cowboys from Newton's cow camp, who'd come over to the far side of town with him. They had a lumpy figure upon the ground between them. They hissed to attract Claude's attention and frantically flagged for him to come over, using their gun arms to signal with.

They had a Mexican, one of the cowboys

explained while he also stuffed his shirt back into his trousers. Evidently there'd been quite a scuffle. "We heard his horse out there, walking along real soft and easy-like, so we hunkered down and waited. We figured it might be a spy, but we also figured it could be someone who rode out with the fake posse. Then he dismounted and come a-skulking in among the buildings. That's when we caught sight of them crossed cartridge belts slung across his chest, and jumped him." The cowboy finished with his shirt tail and made a face at the unconscious man upon the ground. "By golly, he put up a pretty fair fight for a Mexican. Even drew a foot-long Bowie knife on us."

Claude kneeled, flopped the unconscious man over, and looked closely at him. He didn't recognize him, but then he probably wouldn't have recognized the man anyway. He went through his pockets, found only the usual assortment of unimportant, personal things, then asked where the horse was. One of the range riders remained with the Mexican while the other one took Claude out between some rickety old abandoned sheds and showed him a tethered horse carrying one of those Mexican saddles with their enormous horns and split seats. There was a carbine in the boot, a bedroll aft of the cantle, and a small set of ornate saddlebags with some tortillas, extra ammunition, and four carefully wrapped tamales in them.

Undoubtedly the man they'd captured was one

of Bríon's reinforcements. He was equipped like any Mexican cowboy, who, when the occasion demanded, also became a guerilla raider.

Claude returned. The captive was sitting up, probing the top of his head where he'd evidently been clubbed down with a pistol. When Rainey kneeled, the man's jet-black eyes fell upon his badge, and rolled upward to the tough, seamed, and uncompromising face above. Claude and the two kneeling cowboys saw the Mexican's eyes turn slowly, fatalistically dark and muddy as despair gripped the man.

In English one of the range riders asked the Mexican his name. He turned a perfectly blank look upon his interrogator. Claude asked the man in Spanish how many others had come up out of Mexico with him. In the same language the prisoner said twenty-five. Claude pursed his lips; it was a larger number than he'd anticipated. He then asked where Bríon now was, with his little army. The Mexican pointed straight west, not northwest as Claude had thought he might point. One more question: "Is Bríon going to attack this town?"

The Mexican dropped his arm and also dropped his eyes. Indian-like, having decided he'd said all he had to say, and also assuming he was now to be killed in any case, he simply sat there all limp and beaten.

Claude asked once more if Bríon meant to attack. When he got no answer, the cowboy nearest lifted out his six-gun, pointed and cocked it. The Mexican lifted his face, gazed at the weapon, gazed at the face of the man holding it, and slumped again.

"Put the gun away," said Claude in Spanish, for the Mexican's benefit, then repeated it in English for the cowboy's sake. He then reached over and tapped the captive on his chest. "Answer my question, little one," he said in Spanish. "You're not going to be shot. Just answer. Does Fernando Brion mean to assault this place?"

The Mexican raised his black eyes to search Claude's face for some sign of deceit. Evidently he found none because he answered, finally: "*Sí, señor*, only he believes you are out looking for us. We had some spies out and they came upon this party of armed men riding back and forth in the night as though hunting us."

"And you, little one, what of you?"

"I was sent ahead to find out whether you had sentinels guarding your town. If I found this not to be so, I was to give the call of an owl." The Mexican raised and pointed one last time toward the west. "They are waiting out there, perhaps a half mile. Perhaps a full mile."

Claude stood up, looking westerly. "One of you take him down to the jailhouse and lock him in with the other one." He handed over his keys and looked at the other cowboy. "Trot southward and pass the word. Trouble is on the way."

Chapter Sixteen

Claude waited nearly half an hour. He was reluctant to make the owl call anyway, whether everyone was prepared or not. No one, except perhaps professional soldiers, enjoyed seeing a battle start, and if they are the men who have to stand there and swap lead with an enemy, even professional soldiers aren't eager.

The cowboy who'd jailed the captive returned. He told Claude the other Mexican, already in the cell, greeted the newcomer like a long-lost friend. The cowboy also said that although he couldn't understand much Spanish, he made it out several times when the incarcerated one told the newcomer the *yanquis* did not mean to shoot them after all.

The second cowboy also returned. He reported that everyone was warned and ready. Claude listened to the night. There wasn't a sound anywhere. Even the corralled animals out back of some nearby houses were quiet. Earlier, a little fice inside a picket fence had yapped ceaselessly, but even he was silent now. Claude left the pair of cowboys walking out beyond the last building upon the dusty desert. He cupped his hands, raised his head, and gave the repetitive, haunting cry of the burrowing little desert owl, stood a moment in waiting silence, then repeated the sound, dropped his hands, and stood briefly before turning and starting back. He'd neglected to ascertain from the prisoner whether Bríon was to answer back or not.

It didn't really matter; he'd given the all-clear signal and that was what mattered. Bríon would come now. When he saw the waiting pair of cowboys, he growled for them to get back to their places and pass the word for everyone to keep both eyes wide open.

It was both a long and grueling wait. Try as he might, Claude could detect no sound out there upon the westerly desert. He began to worry, very naturally, because he wasn't up against just some two-bit renegade from south of the border, or some gold-hungry outlaw from above it. Bríon was a man who planned big, a man who thought in terms of toppling governments and armed nations.

A drowsy mourning dove whimpered to the northwest. Another mourning dove answered it from the southwest. Claude stiffened. They were coming now, but as he had not anticipated, they were coming on foot. That made him more uneasy than ever. The normal way for Mexican guerillas to arrive in an enemy town was with their plunging horses on a loose rein, with shouts of peril upon their lips, and a blazing gun in at least one hand. Sometimes they hit like a whirlwind, guiding mounts with their knees and shooting indiscriminately with both hands.

This attack, Claude thought, was more Indian-like than Mexican-like. But he didn't long speculate on that; the prize, in Fernando Bríon's eyes, was more than enough incentive to use every ruse, every deceit, each tactic that was likely to succeed.

A carbine cracked southward, then, to Claude's surprise, two guns opened up over on the east side of town. There was a very short lull before several more guns opened up across town to the east where Newton Douglas had his men strung out. For a moment longer that brisk, stubborn exchange continued, then it dwindled off into another little period of quiet.

Claude stepped back and trotted over as far as the main roadway. He thought that eastward gunfire was coming from out behind Barney's store, and that of course gave him a fresh line of speculation. Inside the store, in a gloomy corner of Barney's old office, stood the big steel safe with Clayton's cache inside it.

Bríon would have heard by now that the cache in that old *jacal* south of town had been cleaned out. It wouldn't be very hard for him to know the rest, either. Anyone, including transient Mexicans passing through Springville, would know about the only steel strongbox in town.

Bríon, Claude told himself bleakly, was every

bit as shrewd an opponent as any lawman would want. Perhaps even too shrewd.

He turned as Arch Clayton emerged from the night alongside him, also peering over across toward the east side of town. "He knows where it is," murmured the younger man. "I wish to hell we had twenty more men."

"While you're wishing," muttered disgruntled Sheriff Rainey, "make it a hundred."

Gunfire erupted again to the southwest. It crackled back and forth, then began shifting farther southward. Claude turned to go back into the eastward alleyway. Arch Clayton headed back for the northern end of town where, thus far, Brion had not attacked. He seemed to be probing for an opening, but there could be little doubt but that he had his best attackers over along the east side of town.

Someone southward yelled—"Push 'em back!"— and the gunfire stepped up, crackling up and down the lower end of town. Claude thought it had been Mather who'd yelled out in strong anger, and swore to himself. He didn't want any of the men to carry the fight too far forward on to the desert for fear Brion, who was more experienced at this sort of thing than Claude or any of the other defenders, might pull a quick ruse, then duck into town through the gap left in their defensive line.

He listened anxiously to the angry gunfire

coming up from the south, and breathed a little easier when it began to slacken off, to dwindle down as Brion's men faded out in the yonder darkness, leaving the defenders no more worthwhile targets. He heard Newt Douglas's growl down there, in the ensuing silence, warning his men to stand fast, not to try and chase the Mexicans.

The fighting over on the east side of town began again, but in dead earnest this time, as evidently Brion led all his men around there. Claude heard the yelling out upon the desert amid the gunfire. Brion's men were hooting and cursing and shouting grisly threats the way Mexican guerillas normally did, and while this no doubt contributed much to their successes among poorly defended towns and terrified people below the border, in Springville, Claude knew perfectly well, it would have no such effect at all.

But he worried nonetheless as Brion's men stepped up the gunfire until it was one long, deafening crash and rattle of deadly sound. Some dogs in town were excitedly barking but otherwise the houses and stores were as still as death while people crouched low and swore, or patiently waited, or prayed, if that was their way under fierce adversity.

Arch Clayton evidently stripped his northerly line and reinforced the easterly defenders. At least that's what Claude thought as he began to hear the increasing gunfire among the buildings over there. That worried him some more. Bríon would know these fresh fighters had come from somewhere, either north or south. He just might try breaking into town from a fresh direction.

Bríon did, but he made the wrong guess. He suddenly drew back and hurled his men at the south end of town. Mather's booming roar rang out. So did the excited profanity of Newt Douglas as he ordered his men to hold fast as they poured a withering fire into the attackers.

Claude used this pitched battle to race across, find Arch's men, and order them to get back up to the north end of town again. He made that trip none too soon, for as quickly as Bríon guessed he'd made a wrong guess, he sucked back and led his men northward.

Claude was back on the east side of the roadway, panting, when he heard the firing up north begin to swell and roar. He spat dust and headed on out where his own line was standing ready.

The firing suddenly stopped, but at the south end of town someone fired off one lone shot and got back a fierce string of invective followed by a man's name. Claude strained to hear, then several other men shouted in what sounded to the sheriff like relief and pleasure. He caught some of the louder words being bandied back and forth down there—the decoy posse was returning!

One of Claude's men slipped back to relate what was happening. Claude nodded, and sent the man back to his position. Afterward, he fished out his makings and worked up a cigarette that he popped between his lips but never lighted. He was beginning to feel a little better. Those decoy posse men were badly needed.

Now there came a long lull. It lasted nearly twenty minutes. Claude used it to make a circuit of the town. Newt Douglas had one man slightly wounded. He also had some hard comments to make about the attackers.

"They're good shots, Claude. We have to stay down most of the time and even then they come uncomfortably close."

He went up the east side and found two more injured. He also met some of the returned posse men who told him they'd almost blundered into the Mexicans and renegade border gunmen when the latter were shifting from the south end of town to the north end.

Up north where the last exchange had taken place, he found Arch Clayton with an injured left arm. "Some damned good shots out there," Arch said, as one of the townsmen worked at bandaging the injury. At the look of concern on Claude's face the younger man made a grim little smile. "Just a scratch, but close enough to make me dive like a prairie dog, Sheriff." Clayton jutted with his chin. "They're still out there, but I figure Mister Bríon's had a bellyful for right now. He's probably lost a man or two himself, and he'll have some grumbling to put up with if he led his men down here believing that decoy posse was you out there, and this town was helpless."

Claude flung down his unlighted cigarette and stood with Arch Clayton in the blackness of a shed's heavy shadow, gazing out where the stage road ran, pale and crooked, up through the desert until it blended with the far-off night.

"I could use a drink," he said casually.

"Or that hundred men you spoke of a while back," rejoined Clayton. "Well, it's still up to Mister Bríon."

Claude nodded, thinking he'd cheerfully sacrifice that drink he needed, and all the drinks he'd take for the next year or two, just to be able to hear what Bríon was planning next. "Keep a close watch," he said, and went ambling back down the alleyway toward his own eastern side of Springville.

Some of his defenders were shifting positions, seeking more protected places to take up their positions. One of them walked back to show Claude a shattered carbine stock. All the towns-man had to say about his close call was that someone—probably those damned Mexicans out there—owed him $11 cash dollars for that gun because he'd only bought it the year before to go buck hunting with, and hadn't used it since.

Claude studied the sky to guess the time. It was past midnight. He made another smoke, and stepped around inside an old shed that smelled overpoweringly of goats to light it, deeply inhaled, exhaled, and slouched in the doorway, running Brion's alternatives over in his mind. He tried to imagine what an experienced Mexican brigand chieftain would do under these circumstances, and failed totally. He wondered what he himself might do, and decided he'd makeone furious mounted charge from the east, attempt to break through over there, then, while most of his men were holding, he'd break into Barney's store and try getting that safe open.

It turned out to be a good guess, but as he'd frankly admitted to himself, because he wasn't a seasoned guerilla chieftain, he overlooked one thing, and it happened while he was standing there like all the other defenders, waiting for the next blow to strike.

Gunfire erupted abruptly to the west, but Brion's men had apparently belly-crawled because they were uncomfortably close when they lashed out with bluish lances of carbine flame, when the order came to open up. One of Claude's men who might have thought he'd heard something out there and had stepped clear for a better audition, dropped his carbine and went over backward with a slug straight through the heart from front to back.

Claude saw that, and ran ahead to drag the man to safety. Another man got there first, scooped up the man, and sprinted away with him. Claude fired from low across his body as he also ran along, covering this man's escape. They got inside an old barn and found the man they'd risked their lives for was dead.

Then came the wild roar of massed gunfire from the east, and in a flash Claude understood that one thing he'd overlooked. Bríon's men to the west were only a diversion. The sledge-hammer blow fell furiously from the east.

Over there the fighting became savage and general. Men's shouts in two languages were angrily punctuated by rolls of gunfire. Claude sprang up, shouted for the man in the old barn with him to come along, and ran hard through back lots and between buildings out into the main roadway. He didn't even pause to make sure it was safe to cross over, but raced ahead with that townsman at his heels. They got between two buildings when lead began striking all around them. From here, because they dared not continue, Claude yelled for his companion to turn back and head up the roadway toward the nearest vacant plot of ground. They were both out of breath by the time they got up there where a man might duck at least and maneuver a little to avoid being hit.

Arch Clayton again sent men southward and westward. They came rushing down just as Claude and his companion got out back. The Mexicans and their *gringo* hirelings were coming on steadily, but they weren't mounted as Claude half expected.

He kneeled, setting an example for his companion as well as for Clayton's men, fired at muzzle blasts, levered up, and fired again. All along the stubborn line of defenders other men were doing the same. It was a deafening, wild battle that lasted a full five minutes, and at its apex the line of defenders reeled from the close-firing, but Claude swore at them, making them heed his enraged shouts to stand firm.

Gradually, because something had to give, the Mexicans began falling back. Flesh and bone could not stand up to that kind of punishment. Gradually too, the attackers slackened their firing. The men on the east side of town had won out. They had repulsed Bríon's furious onslaught.

Chapter Seventeen

Newton Douglas came up, and so did Arch Clayton. Apparently Clayton had come down the east side of town personally, to aid in the fighting, for the moment he saw Claude's anxious expression, he said: "Don't fret any, Sheriff. The others I had down here went back to their northerly positions. I'm the only one down here now, out of my crew."

The three of them had a smoke, went back to the rear wall of Whitsun's store, sank down in total blackness, and had very little to say to one another for a while. Over where the defenders still hunkered, waiting for the next assault—which didn't come—men lit up and smoked, too.

"He pulled 'way back this time," said Claude. "Y'know, I think if the damned fool had used horses in that charge he'd have ridden right over the top of us."

"Better to lose a few men and maybe get knocked back once or twice," observed Newt shrewdly, "than get half his horses killed and have to walk back to Mexico."

Claude said: "Arch, how's the wound?"

"All right, Sheriff. As I told you, it's only a little gouge." Arch was sitting there, listening. Around them the town was no longer silent, and yet the sounds were small, almost furtive. Men were looking after their injured companions and dragging their defunct friends back out of the way. Here and there, too, others were going carefully around among the defenders with pitchers of coffee and tin platters of food. Where all this came from was anyone's guess, but without any question of a doubt the women were inside in the dark, working, too.

Newt departed first. He said he was uneasy about his line to the south. Arch and Claude sat a while longer. The sheriff said when the U.S. government heard of this attack upon an Arizona town by Mexican guerillas from south of the border there would be hell to pay.

Arch, who didn't know the countryside very well, asked where the nearest cavalry detachment was posted. Claude just shook his head over that, and said: "Too far, Arch. Much too far . . . even if we could get word to 'em . . . which we can't."

A man passed by handing out tin mugs of coffee. Claude sipped his, found the stuff bitter as gall and as hot as the clinkers from hell, and right away began feeling better. He told Arch that if Brion wasn't pulling out now, then he was hatching some new-fangled meanness. Arch murmured agree-ment and thought quietly for a while, until he'd finished his coffee, then spoke again, his voice soft, his words carefully selected.

"Claude, Bríon's going to come back around to the east. Maybe next time he'll belly-crawl right up among us like the redskins'd do. Or rush us on horseback. But whatever he does, he's got to keep attacking over by the general store because that's his objective, and everything else he does around town is simply a waste of men and time."

Claude agreed. "All right. That isn't what's on your mind. Speak up."

"Take half the men from the north and half from the south. Have your men to the west spread out thinner than they already are to make up for stripping the other positions, then let's not crouch back here like a bunch of scairt Navajos. Let's creep out onto the desert and push our line maybe four, five hundred feet so the next time he comes, we can bowl him over when he doesn't expect even to hear us. Claude, that belly-crawling in the desert is about as silent as a man can get. We've got to surprise him at close range. Just once, that's all it'd take. Just one steady volley from maybe twenty guns, and we could cut Bríon down to size, and then some."

Sheriff Rainey said nothing one way or another. His responsibility was less Bríon and more Springville. If something like this failed, bold as it was, folks would afterward swear up and down it was because Claude Rainey thought he was a big battlefield general instead of just a cow-county sheriff whose obligation was to

183

defend his bailiwick, not try sneaking up on a bunch of murderous gunfighters and Mexican *vaqueros*. He stubbed out his smoke, drained the dregs from his tin coffee cup, and said: "Go get some of your men, Arch, and tell the other ones to watch twice as hard after this."

When Clayton had departed, Claude went southward in search of Newt Douglas. He found the raw-boned old cowman standing in a doorway, talking to a couple of his men. As soon as Claude showed up, Newt sent his companions back to their positions over near the livery barn, and came over to meet him.

Claude explained what he was going to do. Newt gazed at him. "You know what'll happen if you fail, if you get massacred out there, Claude?"

Rainey knew. He also knew something else. "Newt, Brion's not just sitting out there licking his wounds. He's going to try again . . . and again . . . until he either runs out of men or until a bullet finds him."

"I know that, Claude."

"Well, how long do you reckon it'll take before someone with Brion suggests a fire-attack?"

That comment and question held Douglas silent for a time. He, who owned more real estate in Springville than anyone else, had most to lose if racing horsemen hurtled past heaving firebrands into the town.

Newt said: "How many men do you need, Claude?"

"I need ten dozen, but I'll settle for six or seven."

"I'll send 'em up to you," said the cowman, and gravely walked down where his defenders were crouching behind improvised barricades, at the side of bullet-marked mud *jacales*, or were to the west over near the livery barn where it was dark as pitch.

Sheriff Rainey returned northward by walking up the east side of town. When he got back where he'd drunk that coffee, there was a cowboy from over on the west side of town wondering where the sheriff was. Claude sent him back after telling him what they were going to try over on the east side. The cowboy, like Newt and Arch, had glum misgivings. He said he'd pass the word over on the west side of town, then walked away.

A raking blast of gunfire started up along the northeastward desert. It seemed as though Brion's men were edging back into range but in such a manner as to be able to wheel either right or left, wherever the return fire was weakest.

That worried Claude justifiably because Clayton's men were filtering down to reinforce the defenders on the east. Newt Douglas's men also came up to add their numbers. For a moment Claude considered sending Clayton's men back to him. But an aggressive burst of gunfire from up

185

north, sustained evidently because Arch and his men were firing faster and oftener than before, made it appear the men up there hadn't been reduced at all.

Bríon's gunfire then swung more to the southeast, raking along toward Claude's line. He yelled for his men to hold off, to fire weakly, to draw the attackers to them if they could. He then walked down among them to explain, and one of those little lulls in the fighting ensued. He used every second of that respite to urge his men out away from their comfortable shelters onto the desert. The firing started again, and now it sounded as though Bríon, perhaps not entirely fooled by the spotty response from behind Barney Whitsun's store, but at least hopeful, was coming down the desert from along the northeasterly reaches. He was coming slowly and carefully, which made Claude think he must have had casualties in that other, wilder attack.

The desert itself had been fairly well brushed off around Springville. Here and there a tree had been spared the brush hook of nearby citizens, but that was all. Chemise brush, cacti, palo verdes, just about everything else had been cut down and cleared away. The reason wasn't because of any fire hazard; it was more physical—there wasn't a variety of desert growth that did not possess thorns in one form or another. Anxious mothers whose children ordinarily played on the desert had insisted the place be made safe, so it had been brushed off.

This helped Claude and his belly-crawling companions one way—no thorns—but in another way it was no help at all: there was no cover.

Fortunately, that thickening little moon was dropping down again, so the desert, like the town, was criss-crossed with variegated shadows, some long and thin, others wide and thick, all dark and darker.

The gunfire slackened slightly, but it also began drifting closer, too, as though Brion's men, slipping cautiously along through the yonder night, were nearing the back of Whitsun's store again.

So far Claude's men hadn't given themselves away by firing, but some of Newt Douglas's men who had spread out somewhat up along the unprotected west wall of town were occasionally popping away at a muzzle blast. These bullets sang overhead, and that, more than Claude's gestures to keep flat as they crawled, seemed to inspire his companions to obey.

A little ruffle of gunfire broke out up north again, and that stopped Claude in his tracks. He was hoping against hope this didn't signify Brion was turning back to hit the north end of town. Evidently it didn't signify any such thing, for as abruptly as that angry exchange began, it ended.

The only firing now was over the heads and backs of Claude Rainey's sweating, tense, crawling defenders. A Mexican let off a high, blood-chilling Apache cry. Another Mexican let go with the grunting cough of a triumphant Comanche warrior. Several other men out there made the sharp barking sounds of coyotes. It was all done to unnerve the defenders, of course, but it accomplished something else—it gave Claude and his men a fair idea of the approximate location of these attackers who they could not see yet in the pitch black of night.

Claude corrected their course to converge on those sounds and raised upon all fours to motion his companions on after him. They crawled nearly a hundred feet without stopping even to listen before Claude dropped flat; his men dropped flat also, and up ahead where the tawny earth had light and dark shadows, they caught sight of the first gliding ghosts.

Bríon was coming straight in now. That weak gunfire back along the rear walls of town hadn't been reinforced, or if it had, the reinforcements were holding off, but in either case he had to know, so Bríon swerved inward, completing his advance southward, and started his men stalking straight ahead toward Claude Rainey and his defenders. It was a bad moment; they could see those *vaqueros* fading in and out of shadows, widely separated, sometimes halting to listen, sometimes hastening ahead where they saw a spindly little tree or a low wallow where they could briefly hide. What troubled Claude was that he and his men must inevitably be spotted even though they blended perfectly into the spotty gloom, and if only one or two of the attackers made that discovery and cried out their warning, he and his men wouldn't break Brión at all; the best they'd accomplish would be to cut down one or two renegades.

It seemed that this was how the thing was going to work out, right up to the last time Claude moved, then flattened out gesturing for his men to do likewise, and lay perfectly motionless, watching two *bandoleros* creep ahead, crouched and ready to fire instantly.

They came like Indians, placing each foot carefully down ahead of the other foot, carbines held low in both hands, dark faces beneath enormous sombreros almost black in the night.

Another *bandolero* glided in from the south. A fourth one came out of the shadowy east. Those four paused to look around at one another, at the emptiness behind them, then they resumed their stalking, while from farther back other shadowy silhouettes converged, also advancing. It was this second line that held the *yanquis*. It was simple for Claude and his men to mark the distinction. The *yanquis* wore darker clothing and scorned to crouch over; they advanced with carbines at the ready, jaws outthrust, eyes beneath tugged-low hat brims, ceaselessly raking the splotchy land ahead. Occasionally one of them would fire back at the sporadic shots coming out in their general direction from town, but normally those calmer, colder men were content to leave this blind shooting to the more excitable Mexicans. Claude raised only his head. He looked left and right, saw his men aligned, carbines thrust ahead, barely recognizable where they lay blending with the earth around them, and squared around to gauge the distance and ever so gently raise his carbine, draw it back snug, and sight down its short barrel at the place on a Mexican's chest where his bandoleers crossed, at the place where wet star shine glittered evilly off brass cartridges.

Claude fired.

All along his line, behind him and on both sides, other men cut loose. It was a deafening, blinding volley, too ragged for professional soldiers, too deadly for the attackers to stand before. Men cried out in agony and fell. Others collapsed, like the man Claude had aimed at, without a sound. Others, miraculously untouched, let out screams of astonishment or fright, turned and ran in all directions. The *yanqui* gunfighters, though, made no sound. They simply dropped to one knee and lowered their sights. These were the deadliest marksmen among Fernando Brión's force.

Claude yelled for his men to fire, to keep firing, which is exactly what he did. There was no time to aim. There was barely time to lever up a fresh charge after each shot before the gunfighters over there began pumping lead into Claude's men.

One of the gunmen gasped, dropped his weapon, grabbed for his riddled belly, and fell over. Claude's men were turning their full firepower on the other two survivors. They cut them down in a hail of lead. When the last man dropped, Claude gestured frantically for his men to run back into the protective shelter of Springville's buildings. They needed no second urging, but they were slowed considerably because there were three wounded men among them who had to be picked up bodily and lugged back.

Claude was impatient. He had in mind what must now be done, and was among the first of his men to get back where the other defenders were yelling encouragement and gesturing in grim pleasure at the success out there on the desert that the defenders had achieved. Men jumped forward to congratulate Claude. He brushed them aside and yelled for Newt and Arch. All his companions of the outward battle were back among their friends before Newton Douglas and Arch Clayton came trotting up.

"Horses!" yelled Claude. "Get a-horseback! We cut him all to hell. Now we've got to go after him and finish him off. Fetch your best men and meet me down at the livery barn. And don't waste time talking. Just move and move fast!"

Chapter Eighteen

When Claude spurred southward out of Springville some fifteen minutes later, he had Newt Douglas, Arch Clayton, Jack Mather, and several of Newt's range riders with him. He'd sent the much larger force under Hank Smith and Barney Whitsun out of town to the southeast toward Dead Man's Cañon. He reasoned that Bríon, with probably half his men killed or shot up too badly to resume the fight, would withdraw now as fast as he could, and head straight for the border.

The question of whether Fernando Bríon would gather up another little army and return, or whether he'd abandon his urge to get that old Spanish treasure, Claude neither knew nor cared. As he told the others, when they were running downcountry through the still, hot night, the only important thing now was to catch Bríon before he reached the border.

Springville dropped away behind them. Only the rough, menacing desert lay on all sides as they pressed along straight southward on the rutted old stage road. The men were sore and roughed-up and grim as death. Behind, they'd left enough aroused, furious townsmen to fend off another attack upon the town if such an unlikely thing might occur. And also back there they'd left five dead men and nine wounded ones, which made it improbable that if they caught up with Bríon, they would show any mercy.

This was the world of raw Nature, of the unrelenting desert; it shaped those who lived in its hard environment to be exactly as it also was—dry and hard and merciless.

Clayton said, when they slowed for a mile or two in order to rest their mounts, he thought Bríon would be expecting pursuit. He added to that Bríon couldn't have more than possibly six or eight men left with him, which was far too few for him to lose time establishing an ambush to slow his pursuers. Newt agreed with that.

Claude wasn't very concerned. "Hank won't ride into any bushwhack," he told the others. "Barney might, but not Hank. He's an old hand at this kind of work. Used to be a Ranger years back. That's why I sent him with Barney instead of someone else. Anyway, we can't do all the sweating. Our job's to reach the border ahead of Bríon. Now follow me and don't make any more noise than you have to."

He left the stage road where it began to curve southwesterly, struck out through a dense sage field, and emerged upon the far side of it, riding swiftly on a diagonal course that was calculated to put them on a collision course with anyone emerging from Dead Man's Cañon down where it touched the border and flattened out over into Mexico, forming the Tamaulipas Plains.

They had traveled fast thus far, and according to Claude's calculations, even with the quarter to half hour start Brión had back at Springville, they were either parallel to him now or perhaps ahead of him. The trick, Claude explained and the others also knew, was not to lose time but to gain it, even though they were traveling on a diagonal course while the men they were pursuing would be going straight south.

"If he doesn't pick up any sound behind him," opined old Newt Douglas, "chances are pretty good we'll be in place along the border before he gets there. If he does hear the riders coming, we'll hit the line about neck and neck."

Arch Clayton said softly as they began picking up speed again: "And if he does go over the line . . . that's not going to stop me."

Claude looked around. He'd heard that remark. But Claude said nothing and neither did Arch. In fact no one had any more to say for a long while, and during that time the men concentrated on hard riding.

It seemed they'd been riding half the night before Claude eventually hauled back down to a steady walk again, and occasionally turned, gazing northward. Off in the east there was a very faint brightening to the underside of the sky. In the west, night was still fully down. The desert, however, was beginning to take on shape and substance as that pale light filtered out over it. They passed several little cairns of whitewashed stones.

"The border," said Newt, and straightened in the saddle. "Hear anything, Claude?"

Rainey shook his head and pointed his horse on a course that stayed always on the upper side of the international boundary, and which bore straight along it. He rode like that, constantly listening, looking, peering for tracks upon the mealy ground, until Arch Clayton said: "Whoa up!" Then Claude and the others stopped.

"Listen hard," advised Arch. "Real hard."

Neither Newt nor Claude heard anything, but one of the younger range riders with them nodded. "Horses," he said. "But they're a considerable distance off."

Claude strained harder. He screwed up his face, puckered his lips, and at the same time that Newt said he heard the sound, Claude finally detected it.

"Horsemen, all right," he agreed, and at once fell to searching for cover.

There was plenty of underbrush down here, but precious little tall enough to conceal horses, so Claude sent all their mounts back a mile or two with one of Newt's cowboys, and led the others along on foot with just their carbines and six-guns.

"If it's the posse from town," he confided to

Arch, "and not Bríon, I'm going to give up the ghost."

The men finally strung out in the underbrush. Those oncoming riders were swiftly approaching. It struck Claude that he might have been wrong in his estimate of how many men Bríon might have with him. It sounded like a lot more than six or eight riders coming.

Then he saw them as the sky steadily brightened. There weren't any more than he'd thought—mounted—but there were another seven or eight loose horses following along behind them with looped reins and riderless saddles.

Claude was to give the signal when to attack, as he'd done back at town. He waited; he wanted Fernando Bríon eyeball to eyeball with him right down the barrel of his carbine. The riders came into full view, looking tired, vanquished, and gaunt. Behind them that amethyst pre-dawn sky backgrounded each rider perfectly.

Claude arose from behind his bush, carbine up, head and shoulders bunched up around it. He didn't say a word. He didn't have to; those oncoming men saw him plainly enough. Whether all of them recognized him or not is another matter, or whether they saw the badge on his shirt front, but no one could have mistaken Claude Rainey's stance. He was going to kill.

What he did seemed foolhardy to Arch Clayton and Newton Douglas. He didn't have to prove to

Fernando Bríon that Claude Rainey, cow-town sheriff, was Bríon's match; he'd already proved that back at Springville. It was pointlessly bold to do what he was doing—unless his fury and need for vengeance was so deep he couldn't finish the fight without forcing Bríon to face him.

One of the *bandoleros* riding behind Fernando Bríon gave a loud sigh, almost as though he knew something the others didn't know, and went for his six-gun. Claude fired, swinging his barrel just a fraction to get this man. The Mexican sank softly down the side of his horse and fell in a little tired heap. On all sides guns erupted. The hidden men from Springville tried to nail a *bandolero* before Bríon and his men hurled themselves to the ground, but except for the one Sheriff Rainey had killed, no one else succeeded right then.

Claude dropped from sight the moment he killed that *vaquero* and ducked back and forth, heading up through the tangle of desert growth for the area Fernando Bríon had jumped into. Bullets cut here and there, never actually very close but near enough in their blind flight to be heard. Claude observed Newt and Arch and the cowboys with them ground-sluicing over through the underbrush and thought that was about what he'd have told them to do. When an enemy is hidden and invisible behind dense thickets that may hide a man but that can't deflect bullets, the best way to kill without being killed is to pattern fire right through the underbrush, and allow no respite, otherwise the enemy seizes the initiative and reverses the process.

Claude could tell by listening that his companions not only held the initiative, but were not going to relinquish it. He heard a Mexican cry out a ragged breviary. The man had been hit, there was no doubt of that. The gunfire back there didn't slacken even once. Claude was sure Arch, Newt, and the others had tacitly managed to keep some of the guns going while the other guns were being reloaded.

Ahead of him and to his right someone tried a ground-sluicing shot. Claude was certain that was Brion out there, for although he'd moved considerably to the right, and slightly southward, Brion had been the only one of his party who had tried running away. The others were back there, standing fast and fighting.

His enemy tried again, closer this time, forcing Claude to stop, turn, and resume his advance with less recklessness and more silent stealth. He knew where Brion was from that last shot, moved in closer, sank down to one knee, raised the carbine, and patiently waited. Brion moved. Claude fired. There was no great and deadly final combat, nothing spectacular or deathless or dramatic. Brion didn't know Claude knew where he was, and Brion tried to continue on around his friends and enemies alike so he could escape across the border while his men detained his enemies. Claude Rainey on the other hand had sighted movement. He had never, since the initial attack on Springville the previous night, meant to give Fernando Bríon any quarter. He'd for the most part kept that promise to himself, then, when he'd seen movement over there through the brush and he fired.

He walked over, gazed downward, grounded his carbine, and made a smoke. Elsewhere, there was no more gunfire. It was almost as though Bríon's men knew their leader was face-down dead. When they surrendered, there were only two unhurt survivors and one wounded survivor of all that little bristling army Fernando Bríon had led northward, except for Sheriff Rainey's prisoners back at Springville.

Until Claude heard the catcalling back and forth he had no clear idea why Bríon's men had given up so meekly. Barney and Hank with another fifteen men were converging from behind the beaten *vaqueros*. Newt, Arch, and the other men who'd come southward on the grueling ride with Claude, were in front of them.

Barney and Hank led their men up and dismounted, asking where Claude was. Clayton and Douglas had a pretty good idea. They'd heard those shots off to the southwest. While their men were making certain of the dead and mauling the survivors, Arch, Newt, Barney, and Hank Smith went brush beating until they found what they sought.

Claude's smoke was just about finished when they got over there. Hank, the blacksmith, went forward, toed Bríon over callously with his boot, and bent to make certain. The light of dawn was adequate. Hank nodded. "It's him, all right." He bent down, yanked away Bríon's pistol and carbine, tossed them to Claude, and stepped back, looking dispassionately at the dead man.

Clayton and Newt Douglas had their look. Arch looked longest. Up until Bríon had attacked the town, Archer Clayton'd had more legitimate reason to want to see Fernando Bríon dead than anyone else. Now, though, no one had that exclusive feeling, so they all looked at him, glad that he was dead, saying nothing for a while, and in this bleak interval a new day arrived, delivered up out of the desert's spiny east with all the silent fanfare of invisible and unheard trumpets, its pleasant brightness changing the world, if not necessarily the mood of all the men inhabiting the world.

"Did he have a wife?" Newt Douglas asked.

Claude looked up. He didn't know. He didn't care.

Arch shook his head. He among them was the only one who'd been south of the border into Bríon's particular territory. "No. He was a sort of feudal lord down there. I reckon he has kin somewhere, but he had no immediate family. I heard that much in Rosario while I was keeping an ear to the ground to learn what I could."

"Well, then, we might as well bury him right here," tough old Newt stated.

Claude threw his old friend a wry look. "What do we dig with?"

Newt slowly nodded about that. They had no digging tools. "Haul him back then," muttered Newt, and scowled at the corpse. "I just don't like the idea of him lying over in the Springville Boot Hill graveyard with men like Clayton's partner."

"We'll set that to right," grumbled Claude, turning to seek their men. "We'll re-bury Arch's partner with a decent marker. After all, if we're going to name our new schoolhouse for him, he's got to be buried respectable-like. Let's get the dead tied on, the wounded patched up, and head for home, boys. In another couple hours it's going to be almighty hot out here. Besides, I'm about half worn out."

They got Brion like his dead companions tied belly-down with a minimum of talk. It was a grisly chore and no one especially enjoyed it even though they felt no pity for the dead men. The wounded men weren't tied but when the cavalcade turned northward, men were handily placed beside them, not to guard them as much as to be sure they didn't pass out and fall to the ground.

They had suffered no casualties at this last furious, brief skirmish, so their minds turned to the condition of their friends back at Springville. Sheriff Rainey said he thought they should auction off the horses, saddles, and weapons of the attackers to defray medical and nursing expenses for their wounded back in town, and to pay for the cost of burying their dead.

Everyone favored this. Arch, riding slightly ahead with Claude, leaned over and said: "We can do better than that, Sheriff. I'll stand the cost of decent headstones and the best plots. If there are widows, I've got the means for seeing they're taken care of, too."

Claude smiled one of his very rare little smiles. He shoved out a grimy right hand. "Boy, why don't you just sell that land of yours up at Raton and come settle amongst us down at Springville? I tell you, frankly, this is my last big manhunt. We're going to need a sheriff to replace me. After all, I'm better'n fifty-five years old. That's a tad old for this kind of monkey business, wouldn't you say?"

Arch didn't answer. He rode along in thoughtful silence for a long distance and meanwhile the sun rose higher, turning steadily hotter. Eventually, when Springville was again in sight, he said: "Claude, I just might take you up on that."

They rode into town red-eyed, dirty, disheveled, and taciturn, to be met by armed men who stood, silent and motionless, watching them pass up the roadway from the southward desert. Springville had triumphed. It had paid a good price for its safety, but it had also very adequately demonstrated its resolute toughness. No town on the desert could survive so close to the lawless border unless it *was* tough, and unless it had tough lawmen, for in that raw, merciless world of heat and malevolence, there was no place for the weak or the timid.

About the Author

Lauran Paine, who, under his own name and various pseudonyms, has written over a thousand books, was born in Duluth, Minnesota. His family moved to California when he was at a young age and his apprenticeship as a Western writer came about through the years he spent in the livestock trade, rodeos, and even motion pictures where he served as an extra because of his expert horsemanship in several films starring movie cowboy Johnny Mack Brown. In the late 1930s, Paine trapped wild horses in northern Arizona and even, for a time, worked as a professional farrier. Paine came to know the Old West through the eyes of many who had been born in the 19th Century, and he learned that Western life had been very different from the way it was portrayed on the screen. "I knew men who had killed other men," he later recalled. "But they were the exceptions. Prior to and during the Depression, people were just too busy eking out an existence to indulge in Saturday-night brawls." He served in the U.S. Navy in the Second World War and began writing for Western pulp magazines following his discharge. It is interesting to note that all of his earliest novels (written under his own name and the pseudonym Mark Carrel) were published in the British market and he soon had as strong a following in that country as in the United States. Paine's Western fiction is characterized by strong plots, authenticity, an apparently effortless ability to construct situation and character, and a preference for building his stories upon a solid foundation of historical fact. *Adobe Empire* (1956), one of his best novels, is a fictionalized account of the last twenty years in the life of trader William Bent and, in an off-trail way, has a melancholy, bittersweet texture that is not easily forgotten. In later novels like *The White Bird* (1997) and *Cache Cañon* (1998), he showed that the special magic and power of his stories and characters had only matured along with his basic themes of changing times, changing attitudes, learning from experience, respecting Nature, and the yearning for a simpler, more moderate way of life.

Center Point Large Print
600 Brooks Road / PO Box 1
Thorndike, ME 04986-0001 USA

(207) 568-3717

US & Canada:
1 800 929-9108
www.centerpointlargeprint.com